SABRE'S CHILD

SABRE'S CHILD

Catherine Darby

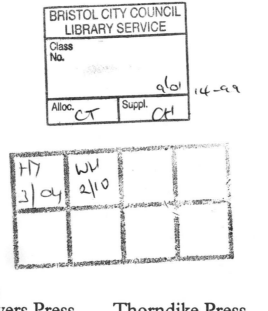
Chivers Press • Thorndike Press
Bath, England   Thorndike, Maine USA

This Large Print edition is published by Chivers Press, England, and by Thorndike Press, USA.

Published in 2001 in the U.K. by arrangement with the author.

Published in 2001 in the U.S. by arrangement with Robert Hale Limited.

U.K. Hardcover ISBN 0–7540–4414–9 (Chivers Large Print)
U.K. Softcover   ISBN 0–7540–4415–7 (Camden Large Print)
U.S. Softcover   ISBN 0–7862–3194–7 (General Series Edition)

The text of this Large Print edition is unabridged.
Other aspects of the book may vary from the original edition.

Set in 16 pt. New Times Roman.

Printed in Great Britain on acid-free paper.

British Library Cataloguing in Publication Data available

Library of Congress Cataloging-in-Publication Data

Darby, Catherine.
        Sabre's child / Catherine Darby.
            p.   cm.
        ISBN 0–7862–3194–7 (lg. print : sc : alk. paper)
        1. Brothers and sisters—Fiction. 2. Young women—Fiction.
        3.Large type books. I. Title.
        PR6052.L335 S34   2001
        823'.914—dc21   00–067738

CHAPTER ONE

1838

Fanny Sabre was on her way home from market. As usual she drove herself and, as usual, the sight of her perched on the driving-seat of the rig had evoked glances of admiration from the men and envy from the women.

In Fanny the red hair of the Sabres was muted into a pale strawberry blonde, framing a delicate, heart-shaped face dominated by eyes almost as darkly blue as the heather that clustered over the moors. For the most part those eyes were demurely lowered but from time to time the long white lids would be raised and, from beneath curling golden lashes, would flash a look of keen intensity. Taller than average, with a fashionably slender figure, she was wearing an outfit that was more suitable for polite visiting than for bargaining over stalls and pens.

Her bell-skirted gown of pale green cashmere was banded with lilac, her bodice yoked with a creamy muslin that matched the long puffed sleeves. A green bonnet lined with the same cream was tilted forward on her chignoned head and her cloak was of lilac wool. She sat upright on the driving-seat of the

1

rig, the reins taut between her gloved hands, a beribboned switch tucked into the side of the seat.

She was conscious that she looked her best. She was also conscious that she had made a good bargain, selling her small stock of fleeces at top price. Her mother would be pleased. At the thought of her mother Fanny's mouth relaxed into something near a smile. Fausty would be pleased at the morning's work. When Fausty was pleased her brown eyes sparkled and the colour in her cheeks deepened. At thirty-eight she was still a beautiful woman though she would never be the lady that her daughter aspired to become. After more than twenty years in England Fausty still betrayed traces of an Irish brogue and when she laughed she showed all her teeth.

Fanny reached for the whip, flicking the pony's rump as she pulled the rein to turn the gig into the lane that wound up to Sabre Hall. The gesture was unnecessary. The pony could have found its way blindfolded. Fanny, however, enjoyed the small triumph of power.

The wheels straightened out again and Belle plodding obediently upward, Fanny allowed herself to relax a trifle and glance about her. What she saw stirred no particular pleasure in her. At each side the moors stretched, rising and falling in billows of green and blue with, here and there, the slow opening sprigs of yellow gorse. There were few

2

trees and the thorn bushes were twisted and stunted by the constant wind that howled down from the high tor at Batley. Nature ran rampant over these hills but Fanny rather disapproved of Nature running rampant. She preferred the expanse of close-clipped turf in front of Sabre Hall and the neat rows of vegetables behind.

She had passed the mill and the long weaving shed where the wool taken from the small flock of Sabre sheep was woven into lengths of kersey. Ahead of her the path levelled out across the grass; unsoftened by creeper or hedge, rose the square, grey bulk of Sabre Hall.

Here she drew rein and sat, the smile curving her mouth again, as she gazed at her home. She had never imagined living anywhere save in this gaunt building and she had never seen any house she liked better. The great sorrow of her young life was that she would never be mistress of Sabre Hall. That privilege was reserved for her brother's wife whoever she might prove to be. At twenty Patrick was in no hurry to settle down.

Thoughts of her brother chilled Fanny's smile slightly. Patrick was proud of his Irish blood and took a malicious delight in reminding his sister of the fact that their mother had begun her life in a cabin on the outskirts of Dublin.

'And came to London as a lady's maid, Sis.'

3

'As companion to a lady. There's a difference,' Fanny corrected. 'And don't call me Sis.'

Patrick always managed to rub her up the wrong way. And Gobnait was as bad, forever urging her twin to mock at Fanny's pretensions to gentility. If only, the younger girl thought, Fausty had stopped short at having one set of twins and if only one of those had been herself instead of Gobnait.

The marriage of Fausty Sullivan to Earl Sabre had, however, produced first Patrick and Gobnait and scarcely more than a year later, Fanny and Esther had arrived. For all anyone knew she might have gone on having babies every year, but Earl Sabre had died before his younger children had been born and Fausty had never taken another husband. For that, at least, Fanny supposed she ought to be thankful.

She clicked her tongue and the pony moved on, past the unadorned façade with its two rows of narrow windows around to the back and its cobbled yard and stables. To her annoyance her brother was there, leaning against the wall with his long legs stretched out before him, a straw between his teeth.

He screwed up his eyes and shaded them with his hand as he grinned up at her. 'Been jaunting, Sis?' he enquired lazily.

'I drove to market, as you well know. You might have accompanied me had you chosen,'

4

Fanny said briskly, climbing down nimbly and ignoring the proffered hand as he rose to his feet.

'Thanks, but poking pigs and hearing how the price of oats has risen isn't my idea of a perfect morning,' he said.

'I wonder you can endure to be so idle,' she said.

'And I wonder you can endure to be so brisk,' he retorted. 'Don't you ever get tired of being so efficient and correct, Fanny?'

'Someone has to get this family to shift itself,' Fanny said. 'Mother won't always be here, you know.'

'She'll probably be here for the next fifty years, so you needn't talk as if she had one foot in the grave,' her brother grinned, shifting the straw to the other side of his mouth.

'I didn't mean to imply that,' she said, 'but Mother works hard herself. Why, she built the mill back up from nothing again when Father died. We ought to do everything we can to relieve her burden.'

'She won't love you any more for it,' Patrick said.

It was a shrewd hit and Fanny's colour deepened slightly as she said primly, 'I never look for reward.'

Except perhaps to be loved more than the rest. Painful self-honesty forced her to admit that, though not aloud. The truth was that Fausty Sabre had scrupulously allotted equal portions of love and attention to her four children. Fanny, for all her striving to be neat and well-behaved, had never managed to win more affection than the lazy Patrick or her sisters, Gobnait and Esther.

'Unhitch Belle for me,' she said and, holding her skirt clear of the cobbles, went around to the front of the house again, in time to see a black mare rearing up while a slim, breeched figure clung, laughing, to the saddle.

Fausty, standing at the front door, raised an arm in greeting and called. 'Watch your head, Fanny. That mare is frisky!'

'It's vicious,' Fanny corrected, hurrying to the shelter of the doorway. 'You shouldn't have allowed Gobnait to buy her.'

'Since when was I able to prevent Gobnait from buying whatever took her fancy?' Fausty demanded. 'Oh, bravo! She rides like an Irishwoman!'

The slim figure, a long tail of darkly red hair flying out behind, had given the mare her head and was galloping across the lawn, sending clods of earth spattering the turf.

'She will break her neck,' Fanny said crossly and took a step backwards as Gobnait, wheeling the mare about, pulled to a shuddering stop and dismounted.

'She's a game girl!' she exclaimed. 'I shall show her at York next year.'

Everything about Gobnait was slightly exaggerated. Her nose was a trifle too long, her mouth a fraction too wide, her skin not merely white but gleaming pearl. She stood in ruffled white blouse and breeches, her head flung back, hands on hips, her white teeth gleaming. Looking at her made Fanny feel tired.

'You made a good choice there,' Fausty said.

'I got a good price for the fleeces. Ackroyd said they were top grade,' Fanny put in.

'Did you, love? That's nice.' Fausty spoke vaguely, her eyes still on the sweat-soaked horse. 'You'd better rub the mare down before she catches a chill.'

'I'll do that now.' Gobnait seized the dangling rein and went off to the stables.

'Shall we do the accounts?' Fanny asked.

'You do them, dear. Your handwriting was always neater than mine,' Fausty said, patting her daughter on the arm. 'You can take the books over to Thomas Leigh tomorrow.'

'So that he can add up all the figures again and get them wrong? Mother, Thomas Leigh is too old to be clerk now. You ought to pension him off,' Fanny said impatiently.

'I can't do that, dear. Thomas has been here since old Mr Sabre's time.'

'Exactly! He ought to be retired. We need someone younger and more efficient. I could keep the books.'

'That would be very unfeminine,' Fausty began.

'No more unfeminine than wearing

breeches and riding like a hoyden,' Fanny said crossly.

'Gobnait is a law unto herself,' her mother said comfortably, putting her arm around Fanny and sweeping her into the hall. Some of Fanny's irritation melted as she looked about. She never entered the dark-stone flagged hall without feeling her cares slip away. Twin staircases rose to a railed gallery while to left and right carved double doors led to drawing-room and dining-room. A fire burned in the wide hearth and there were catkins arranged in a pewter vase on the mantelpiece. Fanny eyed the latter with faint disapproval. Esther would have put them there. She had a passion for sticking the most untidy blossoms she could find into jars and bowls and scattering them through the sombre richly decorated rooms where they usually died and dropped their petals all over the place because she forgot to water them. Esther had the best intentions in the world but seldom carried them into effect. Fanny had almost lost count of the good causes that her twin had taken up and then forgotten about. The trouble was that everybody remembered Esther's compassion in bringing home a stray puppy but nobody commented on the fact that it had been Fanny who had fed it and cleaned up all its messes.

'I'll see to the accounts,' she said now and went sedately up the stairs.

The gallery was hung with small mirrors below arched windows in which panes of coloured glass were set. Sunshine, slanting through the windows, threw lozenges of brilliant colour over the polished wood of the floor and the mirrors reflected them in a series of coruscating images. Esther had a particular love for the gallery. As a child she had often tried to catch the sunbeams in her hands.

Fanny went past swiftly into the long corridor beyond. The bedchambers opened off at each side, the doors closed now. She knew, however, exactly what each room would look like were she to open the door. Her mother's room would be full of the warmth and comfort that Fausty loved. There were books piled on a table by the massive bed in which she had slept alone since her husband's death, a velvet armchair stuffed with goosefeathers drawn up to the hearth, an embroidery frame placed close at hand. Patrick's room was crammed with guns and fishing-rods and collections of birds' eggs that he'd kept since boyhood. Gobnait's room was as much like a stable as she could make it. She had even purloined the old rocking-horse on which all the children had ridden and now slung her dresses across its back. Esther's room was a jumble of embroidered shawls, feather fans, boxes covered with shells, books she had never troubled to read, half-finished letters, bottles from which the perfume had long since evaporated because she had forgotten to put the stoppers back on.

With an unbidden sense of relief Fanny stepped into her own room, closing the door behind her. The apartment greeted her, as it always did, with a trim neatness that pleased the eye and soothed the spirits.

The floor was covered with a square carpet of green decorated with a border of darker, green leaves. A pale lemon spread covered the narrow bed and curtains of the same material were tied back with white cords at the two windows. Between the windows stood a desk of darkly polished oak, its upper drawer locked. One wall, opposite the bed, was taken up by a large wardrobe and a tall chest of drawers with a mirror on top. There were books in a case at the end of the bed and a row of carefully-dressed wooden dolls sat in a row along a shelf at its head. The dolls were relics of Fanny's own childhood and she would not have parted with them for the world. Unlike Gobnait, who had lost the only doll she ever had, and Esther, who had hugged her own toys so passionately that most of them were now sadly dilapidated, Fanny had always taken excellent care of her wooden family, never leaving them where fire or sun could blister their paint, carefully washing and starching their winter pinafores.

Today, without her customary glance at them, she went over to the desk, drew the key ` from the chain about her neck and bent to unlock the drawer and pulled down the hinged lid which formed a flat surface on which to write. Within were smaller compartments containing neat piles of coins and a thick, leather-bound account book. The account books proper were kept at the mill but Fanny liked to keep her own personal record of what she had managed to sell. Neat columns of figures met her gaze and she pulled up the straight-backed chair and reached for a pen and ink. The money from the sale was in her purse. She poured the coins into the palm of her hand and added them carefully to the piles within before taking up the pen.

Of the four Sabre children Fanny had been the one who had enjoyed her lessons. Patrick had played truant so often that Miss Winter, his long-suffering governess, took it as a compliment when he deigned to slouch into the classroom. Gobnait had played tricks, pinning a large notice bearing the legend 'Beware the bull' to the back of Miss Winter's skirt and hiding a frog in her dimity bag. Esther had dreamed her way through every lesson save sketching, where she had displayed a slight but definite talent. Fanny had taken a quiet delight in making her sums as accurate and her essays as neat as possible. Miss Winter had declared her to be a model girl pupil but Fanny had never made her laugh as Patrick did and Miss Winter had never hugged her impulsively as she had hugged Gobnait when the latter ran in declaring she had just taken her pony over a four-foot hedge.

Biting her lip, Fanny made a note to visit Miss Winter at the end of the month. She drove over to Atherton every three or four months to visit the governess, now retired to a whitewashed cottage, and tried to persuade the others to accompany her, but Esther declared the journey tired her out and Gobnait only went when her horse took her in that direction.

The new transaction duly entered in the book Fanny locked the desk, took off her cloak and bonnet and hung them neatly in the wardrobe, and tied an apron round her narrow waist. She took another look round the pretty room and went out again, taking the backstairs which led into the big stone-flagged kitchen.

Huldah was there and Esther lifted a flushed face from a bowl of cake mixture as her sister entered.

'I'm making a cinnamon cake for tomorrow's tea,' she announced.

'Put sugar instead of salt into it this time,' Fanny advised, remembering a previous culinary disaster.

'I made certain of it,' Esther said earnestly. If Gobnait was an exaggeration then Esther was an understatement. Small and thin, her hair of so pale an auburn that it looked almost colourless in some lights, her eyes clear as water in a pointed, pixie face. Her voice was gentle and die-away, and when she laughed she sounded as if she might begin to cry instead. There were times when Fanny feared her younger twin might have a touch of craziness like poor Aunt Dotty Sabre who had died when they were children.

She had actually been their father's aunt, and there was some tale of her being jilted in love when she was a girl. Fanny had never heard the full story. They had only known her as a vague, fluttering old lady who muddled up names and dates and gave everybody wildly unsuitable presents for Christmas. Esther seemed to have developed some of the traits of the older woman.

'You'll need more milk if it's to be of the right consistency,' Fanny said briskly, pushing thoughts of Aunt Dotty out of her mind.

'I'll see to it.' Huldah, who had been housekeeper-cum-cook at Sabre Hall ever since anyone could remember, took over the mixing bowl while Esther moved aside, a helpless look on her face. As it was her customary expression nobody heeded it.

Patrick lounged in through the door, planted a kiss on Huldah's plump cheek, slapped Esther lightly on her behind and winked at Fanny.

'I'll be out for supper,' he said.

'Patrick, not again! This is the third time in a week,' Fanny protested.

13

'If mother doesn't object I don't see why you should,' he observed. 'I promised the Grants that I'd look in.'

'You mean you promised Edward Grant and you'll both be looking in at the Goat and Compass,' Fanny said sharply.

'Which is none of your business either,' he said. 'Save your nagging for your own husband when you manage to catch one.'

'There's time enough for that,' Huldah put in comfortably. 'No sense in rushing.'

'It's all very well for you to say that,' Patrick teased. 'You've been a widow since the world began, but I fret about my poor sisters. At the rate they're going they will either become old maids or I shall have to auction them off at Otley Fair.'

'There's no need to be coarse,' Fanny said primly.

'What a prig you are,' Patrick's voice was as close to exasperation as his lazy nature would permit. 'Always the little lady.'

'She likes to remember that we come from the great line of Sabre,' Gobnait said, joining them.

As tall and slim as her twin she had a casual elegance about her that triumphed over mudstained breeches and untidy hair.

'Let us never forget,' intoned Patrick, 'that our great grandfather would have been knighted had the king ever heard of him!'

'Which is why he insisted that his grandson

be named Earl,' Gobnait said and hooted with laughter.

'I think you're both very unkind to poor Fanny,' Esther said in her soft, flurried way. 'She likes us to pay proper respect to our forebears.'

'Who made sufficient money to build Sabre Hall out of the profits he made of poor exploited natives in India,' Gobnait said, chortling again.

'I'll finish the cake,' Fanny said, pushing Huldah aside and taking the bowl. She was trembling with irritation. This was not the first time, and she didn't suppose it would be the last, that Patrick and Gobnait had joined forces to mock her. She used the spoon vigorously, sending blobs of cake mixture spattering the table.

Without looking at her older sister she said sweetly, 'Be a lady or not as you choose, but do change for supper. You know that mother likes you to wear a skirt at mealtimes.'

'I'll go and throw something on,' Gobnait said, striding through the door.

She would too, Fanny thought with a stab of resentment. She would put on one of the loose, unfashionable gowns she favoured, stick some hairpins in her coil of dark red hair, and come down looking more blazingly alive and attractive than anyone else.

'And I too will make myself beautiful,' Patrick drawled, following his twin.

Esther giggled, then seeing Fanny's expression, became very busy clearing dishes out of Huldah's way.

The latter, with an air of pouring oil on troubled waters, said, 'Your mother was thinking of holding a supper to welcome back the Ashtons.'

'Oh, but that would be splendid.' Fanny's ill-humour vanished and her eyes shone. 'You remember Philip Ashton, Esther?'

'Not really.' Esther was absorbed in stacking saucers.

'Yes you do. He is Sir John's elder son, about our age and at Cambridge. The Ashtons have been abroad these three years.'

'I seem to remember hearing something about it,' Esther said.

'They will be opening Ashton House up,' Fanny said. 'That will be exciting. Why, we used to go to parties there when we were children.'

'Philip was the one who pulled my hair,' Esther said.

'Well, I don't suppose he still pulls girls' hair,' Fanny said sensibly. 'He was a handsome boy.'

'I never noticed,' Esther said.

'You never notice anything,' Fanny said, giving the cake a final stir. 'There! I'd better go and tidy myself. I shall ask mother to let us have new dresses for the supper. It's ages since we bought anything new.'

16

Taking off her apron and hanging it neatly on its hook, she whisked out of the door.

The passage from the kitchens led back into the stone-flagged hall. Fanny hesitated at the foot of the stairs and then changed direction, opening the door that led into the dining-room.

The square, dark-panelled chamber had the air of having been built more than a hundred years before. The carved legs of the mahogany table and the tapestry-seated chairs, the dark red of rug and curtains, the open press on which copper and silver gleamed, gave the impression of an ancient and settled permanence.

Fanny stepped over to the high mantelpiece and gazed up at the gilt-framed portrait that hung there. The man within the frame stared back out of indifferent grey eyes, dark red hair waving about his handsome, half-smiling face. This was Earl Sabre, the father she had never known, killed heroically before her birth when he had tried to save an aunt from being burned to death in a barn fire. Both had perished and were buried side by side and Fanny had grown up on the tale of his courage.

She looked up at him now, thinking wistfully that it was a sad pity she had never known him. He would have loved her more than the others because she was the most like him. He would have appreciated her energy and her desire that all of them should get on in the world.

Her mother, she knew, had every sympathy with her ambitions but Fausty had no head for business. Still she had encouraged Fanny to learn how to keep the books and made no objections when she spent hours down at the mill.

'If the mill belonged to me,' Fanny said softly to the portrait, 'I would make it the finest mill in Yorkshire. But I'll help Patrick to run it when the time comes, and I'll see that Gobnait and Esther get husbands. I promise, father.'

Her promise had about it the quality of a vow made many times.

CHAPTER TWO

'I've had a letter,' Fausty announced and sat back in anticipation of the effect of her words on the others.

'A letter from whom?' Gobnait asked promptly.

'My family.' The brown eyes shone as Fausty answered.

'But we haven't written any letters to you,' Esther said blankly.

'My family in Ireland,' Fausty said. 'It must be about five years since I had a letter from them! No, nearer six! That was when Bridie was wed. She has two young ones now. Seamus and Molly.'

'They're not sick are they?' Esther, who was of a morbid turn of mind, looked anxious.

'All hale and hearty, glory be to God,' Fausty said.

Fanny winced slightly. On the rare occasions her mother mentioned her relatives in Ireland her brogue became noticeably stronger.

'Then what's the news?' Patrick asked lazily.

'Only that Sean and Stevie are coming over,' Fausty said with an air of triumph. Four pairs of eyes stared back at her. 'My twin brothers,' she said impatiently. 'I've not seen them since they were little lads! They'll be close on thirty now.'

'Don't you think that three sets of twins in the one household would be rather too much to bear?' Gobnait enquired with a gurgle of laughter.

'Oh, but they're only coming on a visit. They are only coming on a visit, aren't they, mother?' Fanny said quickly.

'For a few months,' Fausty said. 'There's no work in Ireland, so they hoped to find something here.'

'In the mill?' Fanny looked slightly dismayed. 'Are they weavers?'

'I don't think they are settled to anything much,' Fausty said.

The notion of having a couple of feckless Irish uncles land on them didn't seem to trouble anyone but Fanny. Esther, stirring a spoon dreamily round her cup of coffee, said, 'We must welcome them. It seems odd that we never met any of our aunts and uncles.'

'I can never remember how many we have,' Patrick said, biting into an apple.

'Bridie is a year younger than I am,' Fausty said, looking pleased at the prospect of talking about her family. 'She was always the domestic one when we were at home. She looked after the others and didn't take a husband until she was past thirty. Cathy married a groom—she came next after me and Bridie. Then there's Danny.'

'The blacksmith,' Gobnait said.

'Danny didn't marry,' Fausty continued.

20

'The next one, Mary, went into the convent and Peg was never strong enough after she grew up to be wed or take a job. She lives with Danny. And then there's Sean and Stevie. Mother died when they were born.'

'Eight of you!' Esther exclaimed.

'All living in the one cabin,' Fausty said.

She sounded proud of it though she had been quick enough to leave Ireland and get herself a job in London. She had made a brief first marriage but her husband had died young and then she had wed Earl Sabre and come up to Yorkshire. She'd never been back to Ireland though Fanny knew, and resented, that she sent money home every year and that on the rare occasions she heard from them she became infuriatingly Irish, forever crossing herself though it was years since she'd been to Mass.

'It will be good to see them again,' she was saying happily. 'They were both full of mischief as I recall.'

'I don't think it would be a very good idea to give them employment in the mill,' Fanny said hastily. 'If they're not weavers then they'll feel like fish out of water.'

'They'll find a place for themselves,' Fausty said comfortably. 'The Sullivans generally do.'

'Where can they sleep? There's no guest-room,' Fanny objected.

'They can have the room over the stables. That's never used,' Gobnait offered. 'I'll clear

21

out my tackle.'

'Thank you, dear.' Fanny gave her a grateful look.

'When are they coming?' Patrick wanted to know.

'Not for a month or two.' For the first time, Fausty looked slightly uncomfortable.

'Which means you're going to pay for their passage,' Fanny said impatiently. 'Mother, where is the sense in using the profits so?'

'They're mother's profits,' Patrick reminded her.

'Strictly speaking, they're yours,' Fausty said thoughtfully. 'Your father left the mill to me in trust for you.

'Oh, you're welcome to my share.' Patrick yawned and pushed back his chair. 'You can bring over all the uncles if you like. I've an engagement if you'll excuse me.'

'Which is an elegant way of announcing he's going wenching,' Gobnait said. 'Who is it tonight, Patrick? Annie Holroyd or the barmaid at the Stag?'

'My child, you are far too young to be told,' her brother said solemnly, patting her mane of hair as he passed. 'Good-night to you, my lady mother.'

He swept a courtly bow that made Esther giggle. Fanny, looking down at her clenched hands, wondered why she could not laugh, why she could not accept Patrick as he was, but somewhere in her mind was the hard-working, protective brother she had always wanted him to be.

'Will you play for us, Fanny?' Fausty had risen and was nodding towards the pianoforte. It was odd that, though all of them had received music lessons, only Fanny had shown any talent for the instrument. Tonight, however, she shook her head.

'I have some mending to finish if you'll excuse me,' she said.

'Give it to Huldah,' Gobnait suggested.

'Huldah has enough to do. Anyway it's my best lace bertha and her stitching is not fine enough,' Fanny objected. 'I'll run up and get it.'

She did not, however, immediately run down. In her room she loitered for a few moments, arms crossed on the broad sill of the window. Light flashed out briefly below as the stable-lad raised a lantern and the shadow of her brother mounted on his horse fell across the lawn as he rode away. There crept into her mind an unbidden envy. Young men could ride out alone where they chose. Such conduct would be frowned upon in a woman. Yet there were times when Fanny would have loved to do something wild and strange. She grimaced at her own foolishness and straightened up, smoothing down her dress and reaching for the sewing-box in which the torn collar was folded. Patrick wouldn't be home until much later so she might as well settle down to a

23

quiet, domestic evening. She sighed and left the room with less than her usual briskness.

Preparations for the supper party were already under way. Fausty was making lists of people to invite, crossing out and adding earnestly, tongue between her teeth. Esther was discarding one ribboned spray of flowers made of silk in favour of another and then changing her mind, while Gobnait, her corsets loosened, lounged on the couch and threw in the occasional suggestion. Fanny took her work near to the fire and sat down, bending her head over the delicate lace, crushing down the unbidden desires that had leapt in her when she had watched her brother ride off across the grass.

'The Grants ought to be asked,' Fausty said. 'I know Edward is a trifle wild but Elizabeth is a darling.'

'I would like Elizabeth to come,' Esther said, holding up a spray of violets and trying their effect against the green of her dress. 'I never get tongue-tied with Elizabeth.'

'That's because she chatters so much that nobody else needs to say anything,' Gobnait said, laughing. 'Edward is great fun though!'

'He likes you,' Fausty said.

'I like him too. He's the best seat on a horse I've ever seen in any man save Patrick,' Gobnait said.

'And that,' said Fausty, twinkling at her younger daughter, 'is the highest praise that

Gobnait can ever bestow upon a man.'

'You could marry Edward. He's always wanted you to be his wife,' Fanny said.

'Marry Edward! That's the silliest idea yet,' Gobnait said in her forthright way. 'Because we ride well together is no reason to thrust us into the same stable! I've not met the man who could tempt me up the aisle yet, so, until I do, I'll stay single.'

'Fanny would marry us all off,' Esther said affectionately.

'We can't all live off Patrick's profits,' Fanny began.

'Then go catch yourself a husband!' Gobnait said sharply. 'And leave Esther and me alone.'

Fanny subsided but her thoughts ran on as fast as her needle. Gobnait was wild. She was still young enough for that touch of wildness to be attractive, but as she grew older she would appear increasingly eccentric and her chances of marriage would be slim. Esther too might become as vague and foolish as poor Aunt Dotty had been and what was charming in a girl could be embarrassing in an older woman. It was important for them to find husbands but nobody seemed concerned save herself. She found that she was expecting great results from the supper party. Bullied into a new gown and given a couple of glasses of sherry wine Gobnait might be coaxed into accepting Edward Grant's proposal and Esther must be paired with the newly returned Philip Ashton. The Ashtons were really wealthy and the family itself of a sufficiently ancient line to make marriage into it socially desirable.

'I'll write the invitations out for you if you like, mother, and deliver them round,' she offered aloud. 'I have to go down to the mill tomorrow.' The impending arrival of her Irish uncles was slotted away neatly in another compartment of her mind. By the time they landed both her sisters might be safely betrothed.

She was asleep before Patrick had ridden home—not a rare occurrence, for her brother kept late hours—but somewhere in the depths of slumber was the consciousness that he had returned and her mouth relaxed into a half-smile as she turned over.

Morning brought more sunshine and a fresh breeze stirring the lemon curtains at her windows. Mary had brought the cans of hot water round and could now be heard singing loudly and tunelessly downstairs. She was a far cry from the elegant maidservant after whom Fanny secretly yearned but the girl was cheerful and willing and broke surprisingly few dishes.

Fanny washed, put on a gown of sprigged muslin, combed her strawberry blonde hair into curling spirals that half-concealed her ears, turned back the covers of the bed, and went briskly downstairs. Patrick was not up and Esther's seat was vacant but Gobnait was helping herself to devilled kidneys and Fausty raised a smiling face as her daughter came in.

'I have the list ready. I think six couples will be sufficient, don't you?' she enquired.

'We cannot ask less than eight couples else we'll not be able to make up a set for the new dances,' Fanny objected.

'Then we can have the Wainwrights. I know you dislike Emma but—'

'I don't dislike her. I merely think she's one of the silliest women I ever met in my life,' Fanny said.

'Well, she won't be required to keep her brains in her feet, so, provided she can follow a measure, we may as well have her,' Gobnait said tolerantly.

'I'll write them out and deliver them myself after dinner.'

Fanny ran a critical eye down the list and tucked it into the drawstring bag at her waist.

'You're a great help to me, Fanny.' Fausty spoke warmly, but there was a sigh in her words. If truth were told there were many occasions when her daughter made her feel thoroughly inadequate. This supper party, originally intended as an informal occasion to welcome back her neighbours, was being shaped into something more delicately formal. That meant she would have to be on her best behaviour, refusing the extra glass of wine and only standing up with the staider gentlemen.

There were times when Fausty wondered if Fanny ever remembered that her mother was not yet forty.

By noon when, according to country custom, dinner was served, a pile of neatly inscribed invitations were clipped into Fanny's purse. Patrick, looking as if he had slept in his clothes, lounged in and abstracted a couple, remarking carelessly that he'd ride out and take two of them himself.

'If you drive as far as the Andertons you'll not get back until after dark,' he said. 'Gobnait, if you've lazed away the morning, get your habit on and come with me.'

He would spare Fanny a drive in the dark but it was Gobnait whom he invited to ride with him. She ate her dinner in silence, aware of a gap between herself and the others but, as usual, unable to bridge it.

The trap had been harnessed up when, bonnet and cloak neatly tied, she went out into the yard. The stable-lad, who rejoiced in the name of Alexander, was sweeping out, raising almost as much dust as one of his namesake's armies. She flapped him away irritably and climbed up to the driving-seat, her annoyance dissipating as she took the reins and the pony trotted out smartly around to the front of the house. She was in control now, with nobody to argue with or persuade, the moors spread out before her, the track winding down to the mill and weaving-shed within their confining fence.

Further down the valley the village straggled up the cobbled street, the houses close packed, each with its doors open to catch the sunshine. The breeze blew the sound of the whirring spinning-wheels towards her and she could see, against the whitewashed walls of the houses, the black dots of the women as they sat at their work. Higher up she could see the sheep grazing, their fleeces creamy against the green of the fields and the darker stone of the drystone walls that followed the curve of the hill. Some of the animals were from the Sabre flock, their sides painted with the initial S. The flock had increased over the past few years and the fleeces were thicker than ever. It all added to the profits, Fanny thought with a sense of satisfaction as she flicked the pony with her little pearl-handled whip and set it trotting down the track. The breeze caught the tendrils of hair at her brow and blew them about and the edges of her cloak lifted and billowed out.

She drove with something of a flourish into the millyard, acknowledging the greeting of the lad who hobbled up to catch at the reins.

'Morning, Miss Fanny.' He touched his fingers to his forelock.

'Morning, Luke.' She returned his greeting with a smile from which she carefully withdrew any trace of pity. Luke had been caught in the treadles of a loom when, as a child of four, he had been employed to dart beneath and pull out the spare fibres. Since then he had worked as a messenger lad, slowing him down, but his cheerful manner made people less impatient than they might have been, and he was paid more than the usual rate.

'Mr Leigh's in't counting-'ouse,' Luke volunteered, hobbling ahead of her to open the door.

The counting-house occupied the upper floor of a tall, narrow building. Spiral stairs wound into the room with its high desk and stool and the big window that slanted down giving a view of the weaving-shed below. The looms stood in neat rows, the floor piled with curling wool, the clacking of the treadles muted from above but so strident when one was in the shed that few could endure it for long, unless like the workers they stuffed rags in their ears and communicated by a kind of sign-language. Even with all these precautions many of the weavers went deaf by the time they were in their forties. It was one of the hazards of working in a mill, a hazard that was accepted and seldom mentioned. Fanny had sometimes thought that it would be a prudent gesture to introduce some kind of disability pension but Patrick had declared that such reforming nonsense would have all the neighbouring millowners up in arms, and she had yielded.

She mounted the stairs, unconsciously squaring her shoulders before she tapped at the door and entered. Thomas Leigh, spectacles, which he looked over rather than through, perched on the end of his nose, gave her a stiff little bow, his voice as chilly as his manner as he said,

'Good-day, Miss Fanny. I trust you are well?'

'Very well, thank you.' She spoke with equal stiffness. She and Thomas Leigh were old adversaries.

'And your mother? I haven't seen her for some days.'

'Mother's perfectly well. So is the rest of the family.' She added hastily to forestall a catalogue of enquiries: 'I have brought in the profits from yesterday's market with the bill of sale and a note of hand for the expenses incurred.'

'Expenses?' he queried.

'I had to eat,' Fanny said. 'You don't expect me to pay for my own dinner when I'm on the mill's business, do you?'

Thomas Leigh gave her a look which conveyed that he expected her to do exactly that. Irritably Fanny said, 'Perhaps you would enter the amounts in the book? You will see that the profit is up.'

'It will be offset by labour costs,' Thomas Leigh pointed out.

'The workers have to live,' Fanny said. 'The quality of the fleeces has improved so our next profit will be healthier still. The books are up to date?'

'As near as I can make them. It's not the end of the month yet.'

'They were not up to date at the end of last month,' Fanny said crisply. 'I'm sure I don't know what my brother would say.'

Both of them knew that Patrick never came near the mill unless constrained to do so, but the fiction of his being a stern taskmaster was maintained by them both.

'I'll do my best,' Thomas Leigh said with a long-suffering air. 'It's not easy trying to do everything. There are constant interruptions, you know. The children are forever falling over or getting their fingers crushed and Wilkins sends them up to me for doctoring.'

'I'll have a word with him,' Fanny promised, though her heart sank a little.

Joe Wilkins, the overseer, was a hard-featured individual who disapproved of women in business as much as Thomas Leigh did. Fanny suspected that he used his leather belt on his wife and children and made no secret of her dislike of him.

She nodded towards the clerk, who opened the door with an alacrity that betrayed his relief at her leaving, and went down into the yard again in time to see a small child in smock and woollen cap toddle past, clinging to the trailing skirt of a woman pushing a handcart laden with bales of wool.

'Marion, you're not supposed to bring the child to work with you,' she objected.

The woman paused, turning a still young but careworn face towards her. 'I've nowhere t' leave 'im, Miss Fanny,' she began.

'Isn't your mother at home?'

'Aye, but 'er leg's that bad she cannot run after young 'uns like she used to, and Georgie's likely to fall in't mill pond like as not,' Marion said excusingly.

'If you would all agree to contribute to the pension scheme these problems wouldn't arise,' Fanny said.

'Thanking you kindly, Miss, but we never had brass t' waste on new-fangled schemes,' Marion said stiffly. 'And we don't hold wi' charity.'

'A pension is not charity,' Fanny said and gave up, biting her lip.

It was useless to try to convince the woman. She was like all the rest. They turned down any opportunity of a decent pension but they would happily accept Esther's beef jellies and jugs of soup and never think of it as charity.

'Excuse me then, Miss.' Marion took up the handles of the cart again and pushed it on, the child still clinging to her skirt.

The door of the weaving-shed was thrust open and Joe Wilkins strode out, thumbs hooked into his thick black belt, eyes heavy-lidded under beetling brows.

'You wanted something, Miss Fanny?' He had paused, looking down at her in a manner that demanded a reason for her presence.

'Good morning, Wilkins.' She would not give him the polite prefix. 'I thought I had made it clear that children under six are not to come into the mill.'

'The mothers have no place to leave the young 'uns,' he said, jerking his head after Marion's retreating figure.

'Surely something can be done?' Fanny persisted. 'If the mothers took it in turn week and week about, to take care of the little ones, that would prevent a great many accidents.'

'Trifling ones, Miss Fanny, because the children go where they ought not,' Joe Wilkins said.

'Nevertheless there should be none. The children could be looked after in perfect safety.'

'Their mothers wouldn't trust their bairns to other women,' he said, 'and you'd not find any woman willing to miss a week's pay just to care for other folks' children.'

'But the one whose turn it was could be paid,' Fanny said.

'Paid, just to look after young 'uns! The women would think we'd all gone clean daft!' he exclaimed.

The annoying part of it all was that he was right. It took an earthquake to shift the villagers from their opinions. Nothing was considered worth doing unless their grandparents had done it first.

'Then try to ensure that the smallest ones

keep away from the looms,' Fanny said, feeling outmanoeuvred.

'It's my job to oversee the workers, not nursemaid their children,' the man said sullenly. 'If there's nothing else then I'll be getting on.'

'Good-day to you.' She climbed up to the driving-seat again, trying not to mind that his beady eyes had slid to the slim ankles revealed momentarily beneath her swaying petticoats. She had heard Patrick say that Joe Wilkins had a lust for the wenches and the thought that he might be considering her in the same category made her shiver. She gathered up the reins and drove through the gates without looking back. If she were mistress of Sabre Hall she would dismiss both Wilkins and Thomas Leigh, she decided crossly, and used her whip so sharply that Belle careered down the track in startled indignation.

A horseman riding in the opposite direction spurred his mount towards her, leaning from the saddle to snatch at the reins and bring Belle to a shuddering halt.

'Are you all right?' He had taken off his glossy top hat and was peering anxiously into her face.

'Perfectly. I was quite able to manage them,' Fanny said in amusement and then, as she took a second look, her voice rose in surprise. 'Why, it's Philip, isn't it? Philip Ashton?'

'And you can't be Fanny Sabre, little Fanny!'

He sat straighter, a smile breaking out over his lean, handsome face.

'Only four years older and not so little,' she said, giving him her hand. 'We heard that you were returning but we didn't expect you so soon.'

'I rode ahead to see to the opening of the house,' he explained. 'You've grown into a beautiful young woman, Fanny.'

She felt beautiful at that moment, her narrow hand resting in his, her eyes modestly downcast under his admiring gaze.

'You never troubled to write,' she accused playfully.

'I am not much for writing letters,' he said. 'Now that I am back I promise to give you a full account of everything I've seen and done in the last four years!'

'Which would take up to the next four years if I held you to that,' she smiled. 'It's good to see you again, Philip. I was on my way to Ashton House with an invitation to supper, as a matter of fact. It was intended to greet you all on your return.'

'A supper at Sabre Hall would be the very best way of rejoining the community,' Philip said promptly. 'How clever of you to think of it!'

'Only a small party,' she said. 'Mother thought that a few close friends and neighbours would enjoy toasting your return. Are your parents well?'

'Greatly improved by their sojourn in foreign parts,' he said solemnly. 'My mother declares there is no city in the world as fine as Brussels and my brother, Henry, has acquired a French accent that would make any girl's heart flutter.'

'My sisters and I will feel like country mice,' Fanny said.

'Pretty mice.' He pressed her hand again and let it go. 'I haven't forgotten all of you completely, you see. Gobnait is the one who spends all her time on horseback and Esther is the shy one.'

'And what am I?' she ventured.

'Oh, you are the little one who grew into a raving beauty,' he said gallantly. 'I hope there will be music in the supper party and that you will save two of the dances for me.'

'I shall hold you to that,' Fanny said.

She would wear blue, she decided. A soft, misty sapphire would set off her clear skin and her hair. Philip Ashton's eyes were of a darker blue than her own. Under dark, winged brows they were regarding her with admiration. She had forgotten how handsome he was.

'A penny for them?' Teasing had crept into his voice.

'They're not worth a penny.' She withdrew her hand from his clasp and drew out the invitation. 'Our meeting has saved me a drive. Will you take this for me?'

'With pleasure—and accept on behalf of my

family. We shall be giving some parties of our own, I daresay, when the house has been set to rights. If you ever make the Grand Tour, Fanny, be prepared for chaos on your return. No paid caretaker ever keeps everything as it should be.'

'I am never likely to leave Sabre Hall,' she said.

'Nonsense! You're too pretty to wither away on the shelf,' Philip said, laughing. 'You'll be snatched up and carried off into matrimony before you know it.'

'Not, I hope, until I've delivered the rest of the invitations,' she said primly, her eyes dancing.

'Then I'll not delay you further. Tell Patrick that I'll be sharing a tankard with him soon.' He raised an arm in farewell, clapped his hat back on his dark, curling hair and rode away.

Fanny seldom allowed herself to dream save on her sisters' behalf, but now, as she let Belle amble on down the sunlit track, she permitted herself to imagine a Fanny clad in shimmering white, her features veiled, being lifted over the threshold of the wide, ornately carved doorway of Ashton House. After a moment she shook her head and urged the pony to a brisker pace, but the pleasing picture stayed in her mind.

CHAPTER THREE

It was seldom that Fausty troubled to entertain. Sabre Hall, standing high on the moors, was too remote for casual visitors and, in addition, though she had spent twenty years in the country she was aware she was still considered to be a foreigner and treated with the wary politeness reserved for strangers. Of late, however, she had become increasingly conscious of the fact that her daughters were still unmarried and that, though profits were mounting, the proceeds of the mill would scarcely support them all in the luxury that Fanny craved.

This supper party, held to mark the return of the Ashtons, must also mark the beginning of more social activity. Part of her was excited at the prospect but part of her shrank from the thought of having to make cordial conversation with people she scarcely met from one month to the next.

At least Fanny was happy. Since the invitations had been sent out she had been as industrious as a bee, insisting that even the larders should be scrubbed out.

'Though Lord knows it would be an odd kind of guest that went poking about in larders,' Huldah grumbled.

'But their coachmen might notice if they are

given refreshment in the kitchen,' Fanny said.

'Coachmen! Who keeps a coach round these parts?' Huldah scoffed.

'Surely the Ashtons will come by coach,' Fanny argued. 'The Witherspoons keep a carriage too and Elizabeth Grant is scarcely likely to ride pillion in her ballgown behind Edward.'

Huldah snorted at such foolishness but directed Mary to clean the larders anyway.

'If we had a footman to open the door,' Fanny said wistfully, 'it would be most elegant.'

'I'll dress up in tie-wig and knee breeches and hand round trays, if you like,' Patrick offered, perching on the edge of the table and reaching for a slice of cold apple-pie.

'Don't be foolish.' Her sense of humour, never very strong, was worn away by the long hours of preparation she had undertaken. 'You're the host, and must behave properly and look handsome.'

'Be careful, Patrick, or she'll have you in a velvet coat and the rest of us in tiaras,' Gobnait teased.

'I wouldn't be surprised if you turned up in your riding-habit,' Fanny said crisply, and went out with her nose in the air.

She had mentioned briefly that she had met Philip, but had not gone into details. In a way she was saving him for herself, holding the knowledge of him within the frame of her own daydream. It astonished her when Fausty said,

'I met Philip and Henry in the village. They were buying new saddles and said they looked forward to seeing us all.'

No word of how handsome Philip had become! Fanny decided that her mother was probably past the age when she noticed men's looks.

By the day of the supper the house was as gleaming as even Fanny could have wished. Carpets and curtains had been brushed, the heavy dark furniture polished to shining perfection, the copper and silver brought out to grace the long table and the heavy sideboard, bowls of freshly cut blooms arranged wherever there was a space or a piece of bare wall. The rugs in the drawing-room had been rolled up and the local fiddler was already tuning up, while in the inner room a table had been set up for any of the older guests who might wish to play cards.

The menu was not entirely to her liking. She would have liked to pay a delicate compliment to the returning travellers by serving French cuisine but Huldah had said flatly that she didn't know how to cook foreign stuff.

'And likely they'll be sick of it by now anyway,' she said briskly. 'They'll appreciate some good, plain, English cooking.'

At least the raised pork pies, the bowls of crisp salad, the rolled herrings, and plaits of bread were plentiful, the spread given colour by piles of fruit, quivering jellies, cherry

41

tartlets, and a lemon syllabub that had to be tasted to be believed. She had persuaded Fausty to bring up some of the port and sherry wine from the flagged stone cellar, and the fruit punch was liberally laced with brandy.

Fanny made her toilet with even more than her usual care, coiling her hair into an elaborate chignon with tiny ringlets teased out over her ears. Her new dress was of the exact shade of blue she had wanted, its bell skirt looped with clusters of tiny white flowers, the low neck and short sleeves softened by a bertha of white lace. She had never looked prettier and the sound of the first carriage driving up to the lamplit doorway brought an excited flush to her already pink cheeks.

She went sedately along the gallery, remembering that a gentlewoman neither kept her guests waiting nor rushed to drag them in. This maxim, among others, she had culled from 'Hints and Advice On Social Conduct', a pamphlet written by some foreign author which she had unearthed among other books in the library.

To her chagrin the Andertons were already in the hall and being greeted by Patrick and Fausty. Patrick had taken the trouble to look elegant, his ruffles starched, his hair combed. Fanny smiled at him as she went to stand by his side and tried not to notice that her mother's dress, though of respectable black silk, was cut low enough to reveal the cleft of her breasts and that, in defiance of her long-established widowhood, she had tucked a red rose into her gleaming black hair. With a little shock of disapproval Fanny realized that Fausty was a very pretty woman.

'Fanny, dear, come down and greet Mrs Anderton,' she said cordially.

'I'm already down, Mother.' Fanny spoke with a gently mocking air as she moved forward to shake hands.

Fausty's smile faltered slightly. The rose in her hair had been a mistake, she decided. She had thrust it in at the last moment in an effort to enliven the black dress. Clearly it was too young for her.

Other guests were arriving, most of them being driven in gigs and traps, though several of the young men cantered up on their mounts. Though the candles had been lit the evening was not yet completely dark and the skies were a medley of pink and lilac and gold. The ladies in their wide-skirted gowns looked like butterflies as they moved gracefully in and out of the patches of sunlight.

Mary and Huldah, their best lace aprons and caps jauntily tied, were moving along the guests with trays of sherry. Patrick was making himself charming to a couple of the plainer young ladies. Fanny gave him an approving glance and a slightly less approving one to Gobnait.

Gobnait had been coaxed into a gown of

43

sea-green, its sleeves lined with creamy chiffon that frilled over her wrists. Her brilliant coronet of hair was skewered with pearl-headed pins, but it was already coming down and she had hooked one foot somewhat inelegantly about the leg of the chair on which she was sitting.

At least she was talking to Edward Grant. Esther, on the other hand, was talking to nobody at all. Half-hidden by a large spray of roses she stood timidly, her face as pale as her muslin dress, and clutched her fan tightly. If she were not rescued she would stand there all evening. Fanny started towards her in exasperation but was hailed by Elizabeth Grant who rustled up, mid-way through a sentence before she had reached her.

'—and I guessed you would be wearing blue. I said to Edward that blue was your colour. Didn't I say that to you, Edward?'

Her brother, tall and fair as she was small and fair, hovered in her wake like a large vessel overshadowing a little tug. He regarded his sister with tolerant amusement as he bowed over Fanny's hand, saying, 'Blue is your colour certainly, Fanny, and deuced fetching it looks, but you'd grace any shade.'

'Don't believe one word of what he says,' Gobnait warned. 'He just said exactly the same thing to me, save that my colour is green! In a moment he'll be telling Esther that cream is her shade!'

'With such a tongue you don't need a knife, Gobnait Sabre,' he retorted.

'I shall sharpen it elsewhere then.' She tossed her head slightly, bringing more of her bright hair tumbling about.

'Not until I've had the pleasure of dancing with you,' Edward said promptly.

'Treading on my toes you mean,' she answered, but went with him anyway.

The relationship between them was an old and familiar one. They teased each other as if they were brother and sister, Fanny thought, and wondered if the feeling between them would ever turn into anything stronger. Edward had made his desire to marry Gobnait clear for so long that Fanny worried it might have dwindled into a habit and Gobnait herself reserved her deepest affections for her horses.

'You've seen them, I suppose?' Elizabeth had lowered her voice and there was giggling in her tone.

'Seen whom?' Fanny enquired.

'The Ashtons, silly. You must have seen them. Philip Ashton is grown so handsome! I delcare he has improved out of all seeming.'

'Oh, do you think so?' Fanny spoke coolly. 'For my money he cannot hold a candle to Patrick.'

'Oh, Patrick is very handsome too,' Elizabeth said hastily. 'It is merely that I know him as well as I know Edward and where's the mystery in that?'

45

'If Patrick were to make the Grand Tour and return four years hence you would find him as exciting as Philip Ashton.'

Elizabeth looked faintly doubtful but Sophie Witherspoon was gliding towards them, ears pricked for gossip, and they broke off their conversation.

'Will you stand up with me, Miss Fanny?'

Dr Ackroyd, who was kind and bumbling, was holding out his hand. She smiled and accepted, wishing he had chosen some other young lady. Patrick was leading the plainer of the two Misses Davis and she made a mental note to steer him in Elizabeth's direction as soon as possible. Meanwhile she went, with a politeness that showed her breeding if not any genuine pleasure, to take her place in the set that was forming.

'You're looking uncommonly handsome tonight, my dear,' the doctor was complimenting her. 'My late wife had something of your air. She always blossomed at a dance.'

Mrs Ackroyd had weighed over twelve stone, Fanny reflected with a spurt of amusement, and when she had blossomed she had blossomed into an entire garden!

Aloud she said demurely, 'How kind of you, Dr Ackroyd. I too enjoy dancing.'

Like many men who appear clumsy in ordinary life he was light on his feet and she found herself enjoying the measure as the two lines bowed and advanced, circled, bowed again and began the brisk, tapping rhythm of the dance. No more than six couples had taken the floor and there was plenty of space for the skirts of the ladies to fly out as they whirled down the centre.

Fausty, greeting the Ashtons among the last of the guests, pressed her hands together tightly as Lady Ashton bore down upon her. Though she was not as tall as her husband and sons she had a more commanding presence than either and one sweeping glance of her heavy-lidded eyes was sufficient to convince Fausty that the red rose had definitely been a mistake.

'Mrs Sabre, how kind of you to invite us.' In contrast to the intelligence of her glance her voice was sweetly languid. 'We have been home for only a few days and are really in no humour to go anywhere, but I guessed you would have gone to a great deal of trouble and I am the last person in the world to disappoint a neighbour.'

She took it completely for granted that the Ashtons were the most important guests. Fausty, repressing a desire to cut her neighbour down to size, answered amiably.

'I would have been very sorry if you had not come, Lady Ashton. We're all looking forward to hearing some account of your travels.'

'Oh, my dear, you cannot conceive how tedious travel can become,' Lady Ashton said, letting her cloak slip from her shoulders to reveal a handsome necklace of rubies. 'When we were not being jolted up and down in a carriage along quite abominable roads we were risking our lives on the high seas. However, one must broaden one's mind by travelling or grow deadly dull.'

'Some folk would stay dull if they walked round the world and back,' Fausty couldn't resist saying.

Lady Ashton, who was not sensitive, nodded fervently. 'You are right. Indeed you are right. Sir John remarked to me only the other day that the people one meets abroad are fully as dull as the ones at home.'

Philip, a quirk at the edge of his well-cut mouth, said, 'Mrs Sabre, will you dance?'

'Me? But I—no, I had not thought of dancing,' she began in a flurry.

'Then you must think of it now,' he said firmly. 'Your foot is already tapping and you are far too decorative to be left sitting in a corner.'

The rose might not have been such a bad idea after all, Fausty decided as she took his arm and went with him to the other room. The dance was half over, but he swung himself into the measure without missing a beat. Out of the corner of her eye she glimpsed Fanny dancing with Dr Ackroyd. It would make more sense if the doctor was partnering her, she thought, but it was pleasant to stand up with a handsome young man, and feel young and gay, when by rights she ought to be sitting down with the dowagers and criticizing the young ladies.

'You're very quiet, my dear.' Dr Ackroyd's voice broke abruptly into Fanny's musings.

'I beg your pardon.' She flashed him a too-bright smile. 'I was concentrating on the music and forgot my manners.'

'And I forgot mine in remarking on the fact,' he broke in. 'I would guess that you're a little wearied after all the preparations for this evening.'

'A trifle,' she murmured, seizing on the excuse. In truth she could feel energy coursing through her veins and reddening her cheeks. Philip was here. If she had not accepted the doctor's invitation to dance she would have been the one who greeted the Ashtons at the main door.

She averted her mortified gaze from Fausty who was dancing too boisterously and displaying all her excellent teeth as she laughed. Fanny could not remember the last time she had seen her mother dance but then it had been years since they had given a party.

The fiddler drew his bow in a final flourish and she swept Dr Ackroyd a curtsy.

Fausty, still looking too youthful, sank down on the nearest chair, fanning herself as she called across, 'Glory be to God but that was lively!'

No other mother, Fanny thought in an agony of embarrassment, said 'Glory be to God' or laughed so loud. To her unutterable relief Dr Ackroyd excused himself and went over to chat and she was finally free to greet Philip and Henry Ashton.

The latter, a pleasant-faced young man destined for the church, shook hands cordially. He was as she remembered him, standing in his brother's shadow, never the leader but always the amiable follower. He might do very nicely for Esther who had emerged from her sanctuary and was shyly greeting them. Henry Ashton, being the younger son, would not, of course, inherit but he had been promised a comfortable living and Esther, with her penchant for charitable works, would enjoy being a curate's wife.

'May I claim one of the dances you promised me?' Philip was asking.

'With pleasure.' Fanny felt like telling him he was welcome to all the dances, but that would have outraged convention.

'You look charming this evening.' He had taken her hand and was leading her out onto the floor. 'I guessed that you would wear blue.'

'Then I've failed to surprise you,' she said lightly.

'I hate surprises.' He bowed as the first note sounded. Henry had led Esther out and Gobnait was dancing with one of the Andertons. Fanny noted with relief that Fausty was still talking to the doctor. She gave herself up to the pleasure of the dance, wishing that it was possible to exchange more than social trivialities as they circled.

'Your sisters have grown up too since I left. Gobnait is certainly taller.'

'Did you imagine that we would all put bricks on our heads?'

'And Esther is as shy as ever. I remember when we came over to play how she used to hide behind the window curtains and peep out.'

'She still does.'

'Then we must coax her out of her shell, you and I.'

He had said 'you and I,' coupling them both together. She held the words inside herself, like a promise.

The dance ended too soon but at least she would have his company at supper. The fiddler, mopping his brow, had departed kitchenwards to partake of his own refreshments and the ladies were being armed into the dining-room. There were smaller tables set up about the long table and, in the fading light, the candles made pools of brilliance.

'If I remember,' Philip said, coming with two laden plates, 'you always had a hearty appetite.'

'Not quite as hearty as that,' Fanny protested.

'Eat up. It will do you good.' He gave her such a perfect imitation of Huldah's scolding tone that she giggled.

'Oh, and she hasn't changed,' she said in answer to his enquiring look. 'She still treats us as if we were all about six years old! But what of yourself, Philip? What will you do now that you have come home?'

'Resolve never to go travelling again,' he said promptly and laughed, shaking his dark head. 'No, that's not quite true. I enjoyed the Tour but it's good to be back. It's very good.'

'Will you run the mill?' she asked, and wished she could have bitten back the words as she saw his brows lift.

'I have two managers to run the mill,' he said, amused.

She had forgotten how large the Ashton mill was. Philip had no need to see to its affairs personally. He only had to sit back and wait for the profits to roll in. The Ashtons were rich enough to be able to forget that their wealth came from trade.

'Then you will hunt and go to balls and drink with Patrick and Edward Grant,' she said, an edge of disapproval in her voice.

'I deserve a rest,' he said, smiling at her, 'after trailing dutifully round the capitals of Europe while my mother declared I was the most ungrateful son alive because I didn't seize the nearest contessa and beg her to marry me. She had a great desire to introduce

52

a little royal blood into the Ashton line.'

She was glad he had not met anyone he wished to marry. Something of her feeling must have shown in her face for he put his hand briefly over hers and said, 'Now tell me about yourself. While I was trundling about Europe what were you doing, apart from growing up?'

'Not getting married, like you,' Fanny said. 'Oh, I help with the mill accounts and we all do what we can about the house. It sounds very dull when I tell it but it isn't dull at all while I'm living it. Season blends into season and there is always something interesting to do.'

'I hope you won't be too busy to drive over to Ashton House on frequent visits,' Philip said.

'I shall come so often that you will grow weary of me and order me to go to the tradesmen's entrance,' she jested.

'I promise not to do that even if you turn up in time for breakfast,' he said, and raised his glass in salute.

'This is a marvellous party.' Elizabeth, a slice of cake in one hand and a glass of punch in the other, rustled up. 'It must have been you who arranged everything, Fanny. It all looks so elegant.'

'Fanny always does everything very elegantly,' Esther said, drifting in to join them. 'She manages us all beautifully.'

'You don't have to make me sound like the governess,' Fanny said, her smile faltering slightly.

'I didn't mean to.' Distress rushed into Esther's sensitive face. 'It is just that you do everything so much better than the rest of us.'

'Your sister,' said Philip lightly, 'is a paragon of all the virtues.'

Fanny, uncertain whether or not he was mocking, felt her poise slip away. Hastily she said, 'Why don't you both stop talking nonsense and go and dance? Esther, you and I will compare notes afterwards as to whether Henry or Philip is the better dancer!'

'Will you risk it, Esther?' Philip asked teasingly.

She coloured up but answered demurely, 'With pleasure, sir, if you promise to tell me what Rome was like. I have often thought that it would be a marvellous place to visit.'

'The churches all look like wedding cakes,' he began, leading her off.

'Will you dance, Fanny?' Henry was enquiring.

'Would you mind if we sat this one out?' She smiled up at him apologetically. 'I merely wished to ensure Esther had a partner. She is very shy and needs some encouragement.'

'Your other sister has grown into a most striking young lady,' Henry said. 'If you are sure that you wish to sit down I will ask her to stand up with me.'

'Gobnait?' A faint frown touched the back of Fanny's blue eyes and then was gone. 'Gobnait doesn't care much for dancing,' she said smoothly. 'Unless, of course, her partner is Edward Grant.'

She had lowered her voice slightly but Elizabeth had wandered off to speak to someone else and only Henry heard her. His pleasant face fell a little as he said. 'Oh, I—didn't know.'

'It's not official yet,' Fanny hastened to say. 'I mean, nothing has actually been said, but we all know very well the direction the wind is taking. The Grants are a fine family, and Gobnait and Edward have the same interest in horses.'

'Then I wish them well,' Henry said politely, bowing as he moved away.

'The evening is a great success, dear.' Fausty's cheerful voice broke into her musing. Fanny looked up, forcing a smile. She had begun to feel a slight headache which would develop into a worse one if she went by past experience.

Fausty, seating herself by her daughter and fanning herself energetically, said, 'You worked very hard, and people appreciate it. I appreciate it! Lord, but I was never much good at planning parties. When I was a girl in Ireland we used to hold dances at an hour's notice and then there were always the wakes, when someone died. The wakes were better

55

than the dances sometimes. At least there was more drinking done on those occasions!'

'Mother, what possessed you to put a rose in your hair?' Fanny asked tensely. 'It really doesn't match the rest of your outfit, which is so suitable.'

'For a widowed lady of mature years, you mean?' Fausty shot her a glance that was half-amused, half-irritable.

'I must go and see that Huldah has cooled the wine sufficiently,' Fanny said briskly, rising. The dance would be over in a few moments and it would be only her duty to rescue Philip Ashton from poor Esther's attempts at conversation. Her headache, she thought, would have to wait until she had time to deal with it.

CHAPTER FOUR

'I cannot understand why we have to dress up and spend a tedious afternoon being polite to people we scarcely ever see,' Gobnait complained.

Fausty sent her daughter a look of sympathy but said firmly, 'The Ashtons have been kind enough to return our invitation, so naturally we must accept.'

'And then we ask them back again and so the whirligig grinds on.'

'Edward Grant will probably be there,' Fanny said encouragingly.

'I can see Edward any time—I don't have to trail over to the Ashtons,' Gobnait said. 'At least it's an afternoon affair and I don't have to put on an evening gown, so we may as well be thankful for small mercies.'

The fact of its being only an afternoon engagement had cost Fanny a small pang. Had the Sabres been regarded as the Ashtons' social equals the invitation would have been to a supper party and not to tea. Gobnait, however, cheerfully ignored such subtle distinctions and Esther was too unworldly to care, so Fanny held her peace, determined to behave beautifully so that all future invitations would be for the evening. Her own satisfaction with the recent Sabre party was only faintly clouded by the memory of her mother's too youthful behaviour and Patrick's lack of interest in Elizabeth Grant. On the other hand all the guests had complimented her on the food and Philip had not only danced with her three times but persuaded Esther to stand up with him twice.

They were to travel, at her insistence, to the Ashtons in the small carriage that was scarcely ever used but would hold the four ladies with their full skirts comfortably. Patrick had elected to ride, Gobnait being dissuaded from accompanying him. She had, however, flatly refused to wear her frilled muslin and was clad in a dress of green wool cut as much like a riding-habit as possible, her brilliant hair pulled into its usual untidy topknot. Fanny smoothed the apricot ruffles of her own gown and took a last, quick look in the glass at her face, framed prettily in a bonnet of white straw, before she joined the others.

Fausty, elegant and vaguely unhappy in a gown of steel-grey figured with black velvet, looked at her three daughters and felt, as she often did, a sense of shock at the passing of the years. It seemed only the day before that she had been Earl Sabre's bride, arriving for the first time in this wild, beautiful country that was so different from the rain-washed gentleness of Ireland and the teeming streets of London where she had worked as a lady's companion. Sometimes she wondered where all the years had fled and how she could possibly be nearly forty when inside she was only eighteen.

Ashton House was five miles distant, its handsome Georgian façade gleaming white against clipped green lawn and arched wrought-iron gateways. It was a larger house than Sabre Hall with more extensive grounds, the mill from which it derived its profits situated on the outskirts of York where it never impinged upon the lives of the Ashtons. The property was in a sense not part of the Ashton family at all. It was merely the fountain from which they scooped the means to live as grandly as if they had no connections with trade.

The front door stood hospitably open but the butler who announced them spoke through his nose and looked down it at the same time in a way that made Fausty want to giggle. The long drawing-room was already crowded with neighbours, most of them female, but Philip came to greet them, threading his way through the guests with a genuine smile of welcome on his face.

'I was beginning to think you were not coming,' he began.

'Are we so very late?' Esther asked, her hands nervously fluttering.

'No more than is polite.' Henry had followed his brother and was bowing with every appearance of pleasure. 'Come and sit down and I'll get you some tea. It's a fatiguing drive on such a hot afternoon.'

'Not for me, thanks. I dislike tea,' Gobnait said, tugging at her bonnet.

'Coffee then. I think we can rustle up some coffee.' He looked faintly unhappy, glancing about as if he expected a cup of the beverage to materialize out of thin air.

'Gobnait will drink tea,' Fausty said, taking pity on him. 'She's merely being tiresome.'

Gobnait, looking as if she would have liked to go on being tiresome, took her place at one of the occasional tables set up about the room. Fanny, accepting a cup of tea from a starched and frilled parlourmaid, drifted towards one of the long windows that were open to the rose garden. She had tried, without success, to grow roses at Sabre Hall but the land was too exposed to the wind and the soil too thin. She had hoped that Philip might join her for she made a consciously pretty picture framed in the long window curtains but it was Henry who followed her.

'It is so good to be at home again,' he remarked. 'Travelling is most enjoyable but it can become very time-wasting.'

'I never wished to travel,' Fanny said, 'because I cannot imagine anywhere more beautiful than Yorkshire.'

'How wise you are,' he approved. 'For my own part I am now eager to take up my calling. The living at Batley is in my father's gift and, though it's a tiny village, the actual parish is quite widely spread.'

'You will probably end up as a bishop,' she said lightly.

'I don't look so high,' he said, but he had flushed with pleasure. 'It is my wish to serve where I can be most useful and this is the area I know best.'

'And you will not be far from home, so you can frequently visit,' she said.

It would be perfect for Esther. Fanny looked about for her sister but Esther was still close by her mother, drinking her tea and smiling at some remark of Philip's. Gobnait sat at the other side looking bored and there was no sign of Patrick.

'Fanny, my dear, I hadn't noticed you.' Lady Ashton joined them at the window, her glance sweeping over them both.

'I must wear a brighter dress in future,' Fanny smiled.

'No indeed. Delicate shades are more suitable for young ladies,' Henry protested.

'And you are an expert, I suppose?' His mother gave a teasing laugh. 'I would like to know what a curate knows about fashion—or any gentleman for that matter! Do go and make your bow to the Andertons, there's a dear. They will think you left your manners on the Continent if you ignore them.'

She bestowed another sweeping glance upon Fanny and twitched Henry away neatly.

The rose garden beckoned. Fanny put down her teacup and stepped out onto the raked and gravelled walk. There were stone benches set here and there on the verges and in the centre of the lawn water jetted from the mouth of a dolphin poised on the rim of a fountain.

She strolled down the path, lifting her face now and then to the clear blue sky. Unlike Gobnait her skin never freckled in the sun and the light, gleaming on her ringlets, turned them to molten gold.

There were quick footsteps behind her and she paused, turning to smile at Philip. The knowledge that he had sought her out gave her a tiny thrill of power but she hid it beneath downcast lashes.

'Weary of our company already?' He took her hand and drew it through the crook of his arm.

'I came out to look at the roses,' she said.

'Was my mother rude to you? She doesn't mean to be but she has always had a somewhat dismissive manner.'

'Let us say that travel has not mitigated it,' Fanny said.

'Poor Fanny!' He looked down at her, his dark eyes twinkling. 'Mother can be somewhat formidable, but I would wager on you to hold your own. Tell me, is the rumour true?'

'What rumour?' she enquired.

'That you run Sabre Mill. Patrick says you handle the selling of fleeces now.'

'I get top price for them too.' She spoke with eager enthusiasm lighting her face. 'The mill could be much more profitable than it is if it were run more as a commercial concern and less as a gentleman's hobby. We are overmanned and that eats away at the profits and our productivity levels would be much higher if only everything wasn't always done as it was in my grandfather's time.'

'I can see the Ashtons will have to look to their laurels,' he observed.

'Perhaps you think it is unfeminine of me to take an interest?' she said.

'I think it is perfectly splendid in you,' Philip said warmly. 'I never believed that the sole business of a lady was to sit and look charming.'

'It is Patrick's responsibility really,' Fanny said earnestly, 'but he has not yet begun to take an interest.'

That savoured a little of disloyalty to her brother and she hurried on. 'Not that he is uncaring, far from it! Nobody has a better heart than Patrick.'

'Do your sisters not help?' he asked.

'Gobnait cares only for horses and Esther is too delicate to engage in business, and my mother is too soft-hearted to dismiss people when it is necessary.'

'I would not have called you hard-hearted,' he said, smiling again.

'Indeed I am not, but Huldah says that, for a

female, I have plenty of grit.'

'And Huldah is one of the best judges of character I ever met,' Philip said.

'Huldah behaves as if we were all still children and she had the mastering of us,' Fanny said with a flash of resentment.

'My own nursemaid was much the same,' Philip said. 'My parents too. In their eyes we never grow up properly. My mother still frets if I'm late home from hunting and my father finds it impossible to believe that Henry is capable of a coherent sermon.'

'Henry will preach splendid sermons,' Fanny said.

'I think so too. I am very fond of Henry,' he said gravely. 'Perhaps it is unfashionable of us but we have never been serious rivals in any field. Henry is a good fellow.'

'I agree.' She looked up at him, her eyes brightly blue. 'I would say that Henry is to you as Esther is to me. I always feel a great protectiveness towards her.'

'I would say that you always feel a great protectiveness towards most people,' he said. 'I sense a very great warmth in you, Fanny, a loyalty that goes deep as bone when your affections are engaged.'

'I hope I am loyal.' She blushed hotly at his praise.

'Dear Fanny.' He pressed her hand again and said, after a brief hesitation, 'And you are not yet betrothed. I feared that you would be wed by the time we reached home.'

'I'll swear that you never gave me a single thought until you met me on my way to deliver the invitations,' she countered.

'Well, I've thought of you all since.'

They had reached the end of the path where it widened into an arbour. Long sprays of brier-roses softened the outlines of wall and gate, their sweet scent rising into the clear air. There was a rusting bench set between two great clumps of damask roses, and Fanny seated herself, smoothing out her skirts. Philip, however, did not immediately sit beside her but remained standing, his gaze bent upon her.

'And your affections have not been engaged?' he said abruptly.

'Not until now.' When she had spoken the fear that she might have been too forward made her bite her lip, but Philip smiled at her, the rather severe line of his mouth softening.

'I hoped for that,' he said. 'It's too soon to say anything yet but I'm very happy to hear you say that.'

In a moment he would come and kiss her. Fanny, who had never been properly kissed, felt her knees trembling slightly as she half-closed her eyes. Philip had stepped aside and was snipping off a rose. He turned, bowing slightly as he held it out.

'For a very lovely lady,' he said gallantly.

'Thank you, kind sir.' Disappointment became pleasure as she took it cautiously, holding it between the sharp, curving little prickles.

The arbour was in full view of the garden and the open windows of the house and it would have been scandalous if anyone had caught sight of them embracing. With a half-guilty amusement Fanny realized that with only a little encouragement she would have been ready to toss her reputation over the nearest rose-bush.

'Shall we go back? The other guests will declare that I am a neglectful host,' he said.

'And that would never do.' She rose at once, still holding the rose, her voice tremulous as she said, 'It is, as you say, very soon to speak out. My own instinct is to say nothing at all for a while.'

'Mine too.' He took her hand again, quickening his pace, raising his voice as they approached a small group emerging into the garden. 'Mrs Lowry, you haven't seen the ivories my mother brought back from Florence. Let me show them to you. Esther, you must come and see them too.'

The rose in her hand was already drooping. Fanny went back into the drawing-room and tucked it into a vase of cut flowers, wincing as one of the prickles dragged at her finger and a bright bead of blood welled up.

'You've hurt yourself!' Henry was at her side, his face concerned.

'It's only a scratch.' She sucked the tiny

wound. 'There's no need to be concerned, honestly. Where's my mother?'

'Talking to my father. Father has always had a tendresse for your mother,' Henry said.

'For Mother! Don't be silly!'

'Oh, in the most innocent way,' he said hastily. 'When she was young she must have been a lovely young woman, and the men of our family have always had an eye for beauty.'

'Really, that's too ridiculous,' Fanny said uncomfortably. The idea of any man looking at her mother as a woman was vaguely displeasing, and she frowned.

'And rather an indelicate remark for a clergyman to make,' Henry said, his pleasant face reddening. 'I do apologize.'

'No need,' she said, taking pity on him. 'Will you get me another cup of tea? This warm weather makes me thirsty.'

'At once.' He went off so promptly that the suspicion entered her mind that such affability might become rather boring in time.

'There you are! I've been looking everywhere for you,' Patrick exclaimed, coming up to her.

The faintly hearty tone of his voice and the flush on his cheekbones betrayed the fact that he had been imbibing something stronger than tea. Fanny arched her eyebrows at him and said primly, 'You have been doing nothing of the sort. You have been drinking Sir John's brandy and making love to one of the parlourmaids.'

'How did you know?' he asked, amused.

'Your breath smells and there's a long, blonde hair on your shoulder,' she said severely and spoilt the effect by giggling.

'Little sister, your eyes are too big,' he said, shaking his finger at her. 'Gobnait and Esther see only what's under their noses but nothing escapes you. Ah, here comes your cavalier with the tea.'

'He's not mine,' she began to say, but her brother had strolled off again. Glancing after him she was pleased to notice him sitting next to Elizabeth Grant and talking—flattery, no doubt, for she was blushing and giggling.

'Is anything wrong?' Henry was looking at her with concern.

'I was wishing that Patrick were more like you,' she confided. 'He takes nothing seriously.'

'I am apt to take everything far too seriously,' Henry said.

'An excellent quality in a clergyman,' Fanny said warmly.

'Your sister, Esther, said the same thing to me earlier on,' Henry said, looking pleased.

'You talked to her?' Sipping her tea she looked at him hopefully. 'Esther is usually so shy that it's hard to get her to say one word when she is in company.'

'She is most charming—and not yet betrothed I understand.'

'She will make a marvellous wife,' Fanny said brightly. 'She is gentle and sweet and everybody loves her. It will be a fortunate man who wins her affections!'

'Most fortunate,' he agreed. 'More tea?'

'Thank you, but I am practically awash with it.' She put down her cup and smiled at him, thinking privately that, despite his good humour, he was difficult to carry on a conversation with for long. With Philip she could have chattered for hours and still not reached the stage when she could think of nothing to say. A trifle desperately she said, 'Has Mother told you that we are to have visitors from Ireland? You know she came from there originally. Well, two of my uncles are planning to visit us very soon. We have never seen any of our Irish relatives so it will be most interesting.'

'From Ireland? What do these uncles of yours do? Are they in the woollen trade too?' he enquired.

'I don't believe they work,' she said uncomfortably. 'They are . . . gentlemen of leisure.'

'I see.' He nodded, evidently thinking of them as landowners like his own family.

'They're twins,' Fanny told him. 'Twins run in my mother's family. Gobnait was jesting that Yorkshire will soon be overrun with twins.'

'Your sister has a delightful wit,' he said.

There was a faint wistfulness in his voice that made her say hastily, 'Oh, she can be most irreverent at times. When she is wed she will have to curb her humour and settle down.'

'Fanny, Esther has the beginnings of a megrim and wishes to go home,' Fausty announced, breaking in upon them.

'Poor Esther.' Fanny rose at once. 'You will be sorry to lose her company, Henry, but Esther's megrims can be debilitating. We had better leave at once.'

'Gobnait says she will ride back with Patrick,' Fausty said. 'Will you make our excuses to your mother, Henry? I'd not wish to drag her away from her other guests but it's been a most pleasant afternoon.'

'I hope Esther is recovered soon,' Henry said. He spoke politely but there was less anxiety in his face than Fanny wished to see. He might prove a laggard suitor unless he could be brought up to scratch.

'I had better say goodbye to Philip,' she began.

'I said it for you,' Fausty said. 'He was helping Esther into the carriage.'

'Then we'll bid you good-day.' Fanny gave Henry her hand as Fausty rustled off.

'You spoke to my brother?' He lowered his voice as he retained her fingers in his grasp.

'To Philip, yes.' She felt a blush rising.

'Your answer was favourable?'

She nodded, withdrawing her hand as she

70

said, 'I don't wish to have anything made public yet. It is far too soon.'

'Of course.' Henry bowed gravely and stood aside to let her follow her mother.

Esther was leaning back in a corner of the carriage with her eyes closed. There was no sign of Philip. Repressing her disappointment Fanny climbed up into the swaying interior, and Fausty settled herself opposite, reaching to pat her daughter's hand.

'We'll be home soon, sweetheart. You don't feel sick, do you?' she enquired.

'Not in the least.' As the carriage bowled down the drive Esther opened her eyes and gave a small, secret smile. 'I haven't got a headache either.'

'Then why pretend you had?' Fanny said indignantly.

'Because I could not endure Lady Ashton's basilisk stare one moment longer,' Esther said wearily. 'She doesn't look at you but through you as if you weren't really there at all.'

'I know exactly what you mean,' Fausty said. There was a wealth of sympathy in her voice. 'She looks at me as if I just crawled out of the nearest bog!'

'She terrifies me,' Esther said. 'Sir John is always so kind.'

'It is not Sir John who rules the household,' Fausty said. 'Faith, but there are times when I expect him to be wearing the skirts and her to be wearing the trousers.'

71

Esther gave her pretty, tinkling laugh but Fanny frowned, biting her lip as she gazed through the window at the rolling green moor. Her mother occasionally spoke so coarsely that she couldn't avoid a fellow-feeling with the haughty Lady Ashton.

'At least we need not visit Ashton House again for a while,' Fausty said. 'I am very fond of Philip and Henry but their mother is too much of a good thing!'

'And I too,' Fanny thought, with a small, secret smile of her own, 'am very fond of Philip.'

Under the brim of her white bonnet she lowered her eyes demurely. She had been right to keep any announcement of her feelings silent. Whatever Philip's own affections she knew that his mother would not be pleased by his choice. Childhood friendships were one thing but she would certainly not approve of their developing into romantic liaisons. It would require time and tact to bring her to an acceptance of the situation. For the moment it was sufficient to know that Philip felt as she did and that a promise without words had been given and received. Yet it would have been pleasant to have been able to confide in her mother and sister. The trouble was that Fausty would be unable to keep the information to herself.

'I think I'll walk up the hill,' she said abruptly. 'Will you stop the carriage, Mother?'

'Of course.' Fausty put her head out of the window and yelled. 'You haven't got a real headache, have you?'

'No, I simply wanted to walk,' Fanny said.

To walk for a while with the joy of knowing her love to be returned hugged tightly within her. To recall the expression in Philip's dark eyes when he had given her the rose. She alighted without help, waved her hand, and watched the carriage trundle ahead up the slope. Happiness rose up in her so strongly that she was a trifle surprised at the strength of her own feelings. She had never considered herself to be romantic or emotional, but no sooner had she laid eyes on Philip Ashton after his four-year absence than she had known such a surge of feeling that she had been astonished at herself.

She began to walk up the hill, wondering what anyone would say if she gave free rein to her impulses and let out a yell as strident as her mother's had been. Convention held her back but her step was light and she was humming under her breath as she mounted the rise and glanced down into the valley. As usual the long outline of the weaving-shed, the dark tower of the counting-house sobered her. She would insist on a two-year betrothal in order to allow time for Patrick to become more involved in the business and in order to increase the profits further. It was not her intention to go empty-handed to her

73

bridegroom. Also Lady Ashton would need time in which to accustom herself to the idea that her elder son was to marry one of the Sabre girls.

There were three riders fording the bridge. Fanny watched idly, shading her eyes against the sun, her interest sharpening as they drew nearer. Two men, cloaked and hatted, with a slim, brown-haired girl between them. They began to ride up the hill past the mill with its surrounding wall. She paused, looking down at them, her brow furrowed. Strangers in this part of the world were rare. Only the pedlar was a regular visitor.

The riders were approaching nearer, reining in their mounts. Fanny had a sudden intuition as to who they were and spoke on impulse.

'Are you bound for Sabre Hall by any chance?'

'That we are, Miss,' one of the men answered her, tilting his hat back from his coppery head. 'Would you be from Sabre Hall, now?'

Her heart sank a little as she heard the rich brogue.

'I'm Frances Sabre,' she said, primly.

'Fran-Fanny! Glory be to God, but it's Fausty's girl,' he exclaimed. 'Will you be hearing that now, Sean?'

'I hear.' The other, as like his brother as two hairs from the same head, grinned at her. He had an engagingly freckled face and blunt,

74

white teeth, but Fanny looked at him with foreboding. There was something ramshackle in his manner that perturbed her.

'You must be my uncle?' She hesitated.

'Sean and this is Stevie,' he said promptly. 'Only the devil himself would be able to tell the difference between us but I'll let you into a secret. I've a scar on the back of my hand where a fishing hook caught it when I was a boy. And this is your cousin! God forgive me but I left my manners in Dublin!'

He waved a hand towards the girl. She looked younger than seventeen, her cloak shabby, brown hair limp around a thin, pale face.

'Catherine, is it not?' Fanny made a tentative bow.

'Catherine Farr.' The brogue was softer, more lilting, than her uncles'.

'Named for her mother who's our sister,' Sean added.

'The one who married the groom,' Fanny remembered, and hoped she had not made it sound like a criticism. Hastily she added. 'I thought . . . that is, we were not expecting you so soon.'

'We were not expecting to be here,' he answered. 'But didn't we make a fine killing at the Horse Fair, enough to pay passage for three? So we brought Cathy, for she's a pretty thing and wasted in Ireland where there's not a rich man to appreciate her charm. Now will I be giving you a hitch up to the back of my saddle?'

'Thank you, but I'll walk. It's not far,' Fanny said. 'We are on our way from taking tea with the Ashtons . . . Sir John and Lady Ashton, you know.'

'Did you hear that?' Sean demanded of his companions. 'To be hobnobbing with sirs and ladies now! I tell you, Cathy darling, we'll have you wed to a lord before we take you back to Ireland! We'll be riding ahead then, Fanny.'

He pulled his hat forward over his brow and rode past her, the others following. Fanny quickened her pace slightly. She would have liked to get there ahead of them. She would have liked to stand on the threshold of Sabre Hall and greet them in her most elegant manner.

'Uncle Sean and Uncle Stephen! How pleasant to meet you at last, and dear Cousin Catherine too.'

She would have been at an advantage then, instead of which she had been caught toiling up the hill while they stared down at her from the backs of their hired mounts. The truth was that she would have liked all of them to stay in Ireland and not travel to Yorkshire at all.

CHAPTER FIVE

Nothing, Fanny thought with irritation, had been quite the same since the Irish relatives had come. The girl, for all that she had arrived uninvited, was a quiet, shy person who never spoke unless spoken to. She was sharing Esther's bedchamber, being apparently unconcerned by the clutter that was perpetually strewn around. She wore the most unfashionable, high-waisted gowns Fanny had ever seen and her limp brown hair cried out for the application of curling-tongs, but her manners were gentle and she was so openly thrilled by the luxury Sabre Hall offered that her cousin could have forgiven her much.

The uncles were a different kettle of fish. Sean and Stephen Sullivan were not in the least impressed by the size or the comfort of their sister's home or, to be more accurate, they went out of their way not to be impressed, frequently reminding her and each other of the cabin where they had all been reared, roaring with laughter as they recounted various exploits.

'But Fausty was always one for the learning and the bettering of herself,' Sean said, grinning at his sister. 'She was forever after us to be reading books and combing our hair and minding our manners.'

Her mother had giggled as if she were a girl again. The arrival of her twin brothers had galvanized her into a cheerful and exuberant mood. She had become more Irish in her speech, more flamboyant in her manner since they had come and had taken to singing about the house in her clear, rich voice.

The two of them were too close to her own age to be regarded as uncles, Fanny thought, watching from the front door as one of them took Gobnait's horse over some jumps they had set up. Her tall sister stood by, laughing too loudly, and the smooth turf was being ruined.

'They ride well, don't they?' Huldah remarked, looking up from the sock she was mending.

'They're cutting chunks out of the turf,' Fanny said, biting her lip.

'They liven up the place,' the housekeeper said tolerantly.

'Are we all so dull then?' Fanny asked crossly.

'It's good for Patrick to have company,' the other said. 'There are too many females at Sabre Hall.'

'So you would fill the house with gentlemen?' Fanny hesitated over the last word, wondering if her uncles came into that category.

'It makes a change,' Huldah said.

Fanny sniffed and stepped back as Stevie

came in, treading mud into the rug and wiping his face with a spotted 'kerchief.

'That's a grand nag,' he said with enthusiasm. 'Your sister will do well at York Show if she enters.'

'Gobnait always does well,' Fanny said, a little warmed by the praise of her sister.

'That one should have been born a boy,' Stevie said. 'It would have been company for Patrick.'

'Exactly what I was saying,' Huldah raised her head to interpose.

'More boots to trample mud in,' Fanny said, raising her eyebrows.

'Faith, but you'll be ending up a spinster,' Stevie said without rancour. 'You've the tongue for it already.'

'I thought it was Cousin Catherine who needed a husband,' Fanny said.

'Ah, she'll make a grand little wife,' he agreed. 'And that's something I've been wishing to talk about. We've been here close on a week. Is it not time to be throwing a little party?'

'We gave a supper party a short time ago,' Fanny said briefly.

'Then we'll give another. Your mother was always one for the dancing,' he said cheerfully.

'Mother usually consults with me on such matters,' Fanny said.

'Then we can be saving you the trouble,' he said and went whistling through the kitchen.

'More men in the house?' Fanny enquired ironically of Huldah. 'We have too many already!'

'A bit of honest dirt never did much harm.' Huldah snipped off the end of the thread and put the mended sock back into the basket as she rose. 'I'll tell Mary to take up the rug and give it a shake.'

'Don't bother. I'll see to it myself.' Fanny rolled up the rug and marched out into the yard with it. A few minutes later she was beating it vigorously and wishing she could get rid of her feelings as easily as she could get rid of the dirt.

'Cousin Fanny.' Catherine's soft voice sounded behind her.

Fanny turned, seeing with a pang of pity that the girl's dress was too tight and too short, her hair straggling over her neck. Her skin was delicate and her features fine but her shabby clothes detracted from what she might have been.

'You should wear pink,' Fanny said impulsively. 'Pink would suit you very well.'

'I was just after asking you that,' Catherine said.

'About a pink dress?'

'About any dress at all,' Catherine said. 'Uncle Stevie says there's to be a grand party but I have nothing fit to wear. I was hoping that you might advise me, you always being so fashionable.'

It had been on the tip of Fanny's tongue to enquire tartly since when had Stephen Sullivan been in charge but the girl's innocent flattery was touching.

'I have a pink gown,' she said. 'I only wore it the once before I realized it was a mistake. I've too much auburn in my hair to wear that shade, but it would suit your colouring beautifully and we're much of a size so it wouldn't need much alteration. Come, we'll go up and look.'

Abandoning rug and beater she set a brisk pace to the house. The gown was soon laid across the chair and Catherine's eyes were fixed on it admiringly.

'Sure but it's too good for you to be lending,' she said doubtfully.

'Giving, not lending,' Fanny corrected.

'It's silk.' Catherine's thin fingers stroked its hem.

'Because we run a mill we don't have to wear wool at every season,' Fanny said, amused. 'Try it on now, and I'll see if it needs much taking in.' Her cousin obeyed, pulling off her skimpy dress to reveal clean but heavily-darned undergarments. The dress would require only a couple of tucks at the waistband. 'And a fichu. Your shoulders are a mite too thin.' Fanny stood back, head on one side as she contemplated the younger girl. 'Your hair requires styling. Sit down and let me see what's to be done.'

Catherine sat, obedient as a doll, while Fanny combed through the fine, limp strands, winding them about her ears from a centre parting. The style suited her cousin, emphasizing her broad, low brow and imparting more maturity to her bearing.

'Now you look charming,' Fanny said at last, pinning a final coil into place. 'I will lend you my brown cape and bonnet and you can wear the whole outfit at the Horse Show next month, if you're still here?'

There was a lot of questioning in her voice which she feared might sound tactless, but Catherine answered innocently, 'Oh, we've no thoughts of going back to Ireland, yet. The uncles cannot find work there, and my parents are hoping I'll find an English husband like Aunt Fausty did.'

'I doubt if there are men like my father left,' Fanny said. 'I never knew him because he died before I was born but he was most highly respected, and he died a hero, trying to save his aunt from a fire in the barn.'

'So, it's your mother who kept the mill going?' Catherine said.

'Well, yes. I suppose so. But the profits only really started to increase after I became of age to help her.'

'You're all very clever,' Catherine said without envy. 'I never had much of an education. Oh, I can manage the reading and the writing, but I never had a real talent for anything.'

'Except for being modest and pretty,' Fanny said generously. 'Most men don't ask for more in a wife.'

'I'm sure I hope so.' Catherine gave her reflection another anxious glance.

She was really quite charming, Fanny thought. If Henry were not earmarked for Esther he would have done splendidly, but there were several younger sons in the neighbourhood with whom she might be matched.

'Fanny, are you going down to the mill today?' Esther enquired from the doorway.

'I hadn't planned to go, why?'

'I promised to take a basket of sweets for the children, but I cannot spare the time. I'd completely forgotten that there may be a—a visitor,' Esther said, blushing slightly.

No need to ask who was coming. Fanny gave her sister an amused glance.

'I'll take the basket,' she said equably. 'Catherine, would you like to come with me? No need to change again—you can wear the brown cape now and we'll alter the dress when you come back.'

'It's in the kitchen. You will see the little ones get a share, won't you? The bigger ones push them out of the way and take more than they should,' Esther said.

'Go and make yourself pretty for your visitor and leave it to me.'

Fanny gave her sister a friendly little push. Esther in love was more vague and gentle than ever. She would have to wake up a little when she became Henry's wife. She took down the cloaks, gave one to Catherine and whisked out.

Huldah, giving her the covered basket, said, 'Some of the sweets ran together into a lump on account of Esther's not spacing them out properly on the baking-tray when she brought them out to cool. The children can fight over it for I've not time to go chopping it up now.'

'Esther is expecting a visitor. Will you serve them some tea in the parlour and see that they're not disturbed?'

Not wishing to hurt Catherine's feelings by mentioning the uncles openly Fanny gave Huldah a meaning look, but received only a brusque, 'I hope I know by now how visitors are to be entertained.'

'Huldah gets above herself at times,' Fanny confided as she and Catherine settled themselves in the trap.

'She frightens me to death,' Catherine whispered. 'We never had a housekeeper.'

'They're just servants,' Fanny said, 'but Huldah's been here for ever. She regards herself as one of the family and my mother is apt to give in to her whims.'

'I think Aunt Fausty is one of the most darling people I ever met,' Catherine said with enthusiasm. 'She's so young and pretty and full of life. 'Tis hard to remember that she's a widow at all. Why, in Dublin, she'd have been snapped up again as quick as can be!'

'Mother would never consider marrying again. She is too devoted to my father's memory,' Fanny said crisply, flicking the pony's back as they rounded the corner.

Gobnait and the uncles were still clustered about the horse, admiring its points. Fanny raised a casual hand in greeting and drove across the turf onto the track. She hoped they would have the tact not to intrude when Henry arrived. Sooner or later the Ashtons would have to meet Fausty's relations but she would have liked the engagement to have been made public first.

A horseman was riding towards them up the valley. She pulled and called a faintly surprised greeting.

'Good-day, Philip! I thought Henry was coming.'

'Henry's nursing a summer cold. I heard you had guests.' He had removed his hat and was glancing at Catherine.

'My Irish uncles arrived sooner than expected. This is my cousin, Catherine Farr,' she hastened to say. 'Catherine, this is Philip Ashton.'

'Delighted to meet you, Miss Farr.' He bowed in her direction.

'We're going down to the mill with some sweets for the little ones,' Fanny said. 'Will you come?'

'I want a few words with your mother.' He gave her the slow smile that warmed his dark eyes and made her wish that Catherine wasn't by. 'I suppose you can guess what it's about.'

'Isn't it too soon?' she ventured.

'For a public announcement, perhaps, but it's only fair that your mother should grant her permission.'

'Mother will be delighted,' she assured him.

'And later I will inform my own family,' Philip said.

'Who will be rather less delighted,' Fanny thought wryly, but the thought was hidden by her smile as she said briskly, 'I'd best get on. I'm sorry Henry is sick. It's not serious?'

'He merely behaves as if it were. I'm happy to have met you, Miss Farr.'

He trotted past them and Catherine turned wide eyes towards her.

'Faith, but that's a fine-looking young man,' she breathed. 'Would that be Cousin Esther's visitor?'

'Only to tell her that the one she's expected cannot come.' Fanny clicked her tongue and the trap bowled on.

'Would he be a real lord now?' Catherine enquired.

'His father was knighted some years back.'

Catherine subsided, perhaps sensing a faint reserve in her companion's tone and they drove in silence over the brow of the hill and down to the millyard.

To Fanny's irritation it was Joe Wilton who came to greet them, his thumbs hooked in his belt, his small eyes darting over Catherine.

'Good-day, Wilton.' She addressed him coolly, alighting from the trap without help. 'Have the children lined up in the yard for me, will you?'

'Holding an inspection, Miss Fanny?' he enquired.

'My sister has made some sweets for the little ones,' she said coldly.

'I cannot bring the work to a stop while you dole out sweets. We lose profit that road and you'll be first to complain if we do,' he said.

'Five minutes will make no matter.'

'Five minutes here and five minutes there makes a deal of difference,' he disagreed. 'I shall have to dock the wages again.'

'Again?' She caught him up sharply.

'I've the right to dock wages for time-wasting,' Wilton said.

'You said "again". Whose wages did you dock and why?'

'Elsie Stubbs was near an hour late with some excuse that her Billy had the croup and she'd been up nursing him. I docked her fourpence.'

'Without permission?'

'Mr Patrick is never around,' Wilton shrugged, 'and I wasn't about to traipse up to Sabre Hall when you're packed out with guests.'

His eyes had slid to Catherine again.

'In future you will make a note of any money that is to be docked and give it to me for approval,' Fanny said.

'That would make my job harder than it already is,' he complained. 'Either I'm overseer or I'm not!'

'Take the matter up with Mr Patrick if you've any objections. Now send out the children, all those under ten, and don't get any notions about docking their money.'

She spoke with decision, her eyes challenging him to disagree. After a moment he shifted his feet uncomfortably and said, more to Catherine than to herself, 'You cannot blame a man for wanting to do his work without interference.'

'The children, if you please,' Fanny repeated.

He stumped off without answering, banging the door of the weaving-shed behind him.

'What a horrid man!' Catherine's face had paled and her voice trembled.

'A brute,' Fanny agreed, 'but he does get plenty of work out of the weavers. But if I could find a better I'd have him laid off.'

The children were filing out, their eyes brightening as they saw the basket. Esther's gifts, though intermittent, were always eagerly welcomed, though her cakes were flat more often than not and she was apt to give out ribbons instead of scarves.

'May I give them out?' Catherine asked shyly.

'Of course, if you wish,' Fanny handed over the basket.

'I never have anything to give, you see,' Catherine said, her face lighting up as she stepped forward.

No doubt she saw herself as Lady Bountiful, Fanny thought with affectionate amusement. She was beginning to like her cousin more and more. It would be a real kindness to help her with her wardrobe and the dressing of her hair. In her mind she began to compile a list of prospective bridegrooms.

'Would that be one of the Irish relatives?' Joe Wilton said, returning to stand by Fanny.

'The young lady is my cousin.' Fanny drew away from him.

'She's a pretty piece,' he said, his tone spiced with insolence, and walked off before she could make any retort, raising his voice to order, 'Hurry up now. Take one and get back to your work. You're not paid for idling!'

She would have to speak to Patrick, Fanny decided, and make him understand that the overseer was abusing his position by his lack of respect and his high-handed ways. Talking to Patrick and making him listen wasn't easy at the best of times, and since the uncles had arrived she had scarcely seen him. He had spent much of the day riding with them and in the evenings he had generally been too foxed when he got home from the tavern to make any sense.

The children were being herded back to work, their cheeks bulging with toffee. Wilton had paused to speak to Catherine and Fanny saw the girl blush scarlet and stammer some reply. She walked across, her tone smooth but warning.

'Catherine, we haven't time to linger. Mother will be expecting us.'

'Nice to talk to you, Miss.' The overseer was smiling and there was a quality in that smile that made Catherine's embarrassment easy to understand.

Her own colour rising she said, 'Wilton, get back to your work. We pay you to oversee, not to gossip.'

'Aye, Miss Fanny.' His eyes raked her from head to foot as he touched his forelock. 'As you say, Miss Fanny.'

'Come, we'll drive back.' She touched her cousin lightly on the arm.

Philip would be wanting some time alone with her. They'd not met since the afternoon of the tea at Ashton House for the arrival of the guests had kept Fanny fully occupied. It would be pleasant to stop being the efficient Miss Sabre and be Fanny in love for a little while.

'That man,' Catherine whispered as they walked back to the trap together, 'has the cheek of the very devil! Wasn't he just asking me if I was promised and do you know what he said after?'

'No, what?'

'He said it was a great pity he had a wife.'

'A pity for his wife,' Fanny said grimly. 'She's a poor shadow of a woman. It's my belief he beats her but she's too frightened to make any complaint. He had no business to talk to you in such a way. He should remember that you are a guest at Sabre Hall.'

'But not a lady,' her mind silently added. Joe Wilton, for all his grossness, would not have spoken so freely to a lady, and Catherine, even with her hair dressed, wearing the borrowed cloak, looked the simple country girl that she was. There was work to be done before Cousin Catherine would be suitable to offer as a prospective bride to even a younger son.

Climbing up to the driving-seat and taking up the reins she said, trying not to sound too critical, 'It is best to ignore him. You are apt to give the impression of being too ready to be friendly. In Ireland that may be the custom, but here in Yorkshire we keep ourselves more to ourselves.'

'Then how does a body get to know anybody at all?' Catherine asked.

'There are certain customs,' Fanny said patiently. 'Rules of society that gentlefolk learn, and people like Joe Wilton seek to overturn.'

'Like Aunt Fausty did when she came to England to marry a gentleman?'

'That's not the same at all!' Fanny snapped.

'I'm sorry,' Catherine flushed again miserably. 'I know that I have a great deal to learn. You will have to be patient with me.'

'Nonsense! You will do very well,' Fanny said. 'In a month or two men like Wilton won't dare to say anything out of place to you!'

'I'm sure I hope so,' Catherine said meekly.

'I shall talk to Patrick and make him fine Wilton for insolence.'

'I'm not wishing to cause any trouble,' Catherine said uneasily.

'I shall speak to Patrick.' Fanny urged Belle to a faster pace.

To her disappointment there was no sign of Philip when they reached the house and entered the drawing-room. Only Fausty was there, immersed in a book which she promptly put aside as the two girls came in.

'You look very pretty, Catherine,' she said, but her smiling eyes had flown to her daughter.

'Cousin Fanny has given me the dress,' Catherine said, opening her cloak to reveal the pink gown. 'It is all right, isn't it? You'd not be having any objections?'

'Fanny may do as she wishes with her gowns,' Fausty said promptly. 'That one suits you very well, dear. You must wear it at the Horse Show. We are to take a box this year and watch Patrick and Gobnait win all the prizes.'

'Is there to be a party?' Catherine asked.

'Very likely. Run along and change now, there's a dear.'

Fausty watched Catherine leave the room and turned again to Fanny, her brown eyes sparkling.

'Philip has talked to me,' she said.

'I thought he would still be here,' Fanny admitted.

'He was due back for a dinner and didn't want to offend by being late. That young man must tread carefully to keep his parents' approval,' Fausty said.

'His mother's, you mean.' Fanny loosened her cape and sat down. 'You approve though, don't you? You're pleased?'

'Very pleased, if it's what you want,' Fausty said. 'Esther too. She had said nothing to me, but I sensed something in the wind. You are both sly pussies, the pair of you!'

'The Ashtons are a fine family,' Fanny said, 'but it's wiser to make no public announcement at all until Philip and Henry have talked to Sir John and Lady Ashton. These matters have to be correctly worked out.'

'I suppose so.' Fausty looked a trifle wistful. 'In Ireland there's not the same fuss. A lad and a girl meet and fall in love and, when they've seen the priest, they go to the church and make their vows . . . run there if there's a babe on the way.' She threw back her dark head and laughed heartily.

'Mother, please! Someone may hear,' Fanny said.

'Oh, I shall be staid enough when the announcement is made,' Fausty promised. 'Don't look so shocked. You're not married yet, you know.'

'You haven't told the uncles?' Fanny asked.

'Philip said it was to be a secret for the time being.'

'Only until his parents have given their consent,' Fanny said, 'and then you may tell the whole neighbourhood. Where's Esther?'

'She went for a walk, I think.'

'I'll find her. It's time we exchanged congratulations,' Fanny said, springing up.

'You're sure about your feelings?' There was a trace of anxiety in Fausty's eyes. 'All this seems to have come about so quickly.'

'I'm sure.' Fanny bent and gave her mother a rare impulsive kiss on the cheek. 'I'm very sure, Mother.'

She pulled her cape about herself again and went out, treading lightly.

CHAPTER SIX

There was no sign of Esther in the yard or the vegetable patch but Fanny walked unerringly past the stables down the narrow path that wound between banks of heather to where a brook sprinkled brown stones that changed into jewels under the bright sun. It was one of Esther's favourite places and, as Fanny had expected, her sister was there, seated on the grass and chewing a long stem of meadowsweet. She wore one of her floating gowns in a shade that blended with her background so well that she appeared as white face and hands against the green.

'Fanny, did you take the sweets?' was her first question as the other stepped down to join her.

'And saw them fairly shared. You look happy, but I don't suppose I need to ask why,' Fanny said.

'I wondered if you'd guessed,' Esther said with a shy, upward look. 'I can scarcely believe that it's happened to me. I always thought that I'd stay at home with mother and take care of her when she was old.'

'You'll make a lovely wife,' Fanny said warmly. 'I'm sorry Henry has a cold but it isn't serious. I'm sure he will visit as soon as he possibly can.'

'Oh, summer colds don't last very long,' Esther agreed. 'After four years of travelling in warm countries it takes time to get accustomed to our climate again, I suppose.'

'He's a pleasant young man,' Fanny said. 'I think he'll make a most attentive husband.'

'Oh, I do hope so,' Esther said, clasping her narrow hands together. 'You deserve to be happy, Fanny.'

'We both deserve to be happy,' Fanny began, then frowned. 'What exactly made you say that then?'

'Why, you've always been the cleverest of us and the one who works hardest,' Esther said in her innocent way. 'You deserve to be happy. Henry may very well be a bishop one day. You may depend upon Philip giving him the best recommendation.'

Fanny's mouth had dried up and her heart was beating uncomfortably fast. Very cautiously she said, 'You are in love with Philip?'

'I didn't think that I could ever feel as I do,' Esther said. 'I was so nervous at the thought of meeting the Ashtons again that I would have hidden away all evening had Philip not danced with me. We both of us knew our own feelings at once but we didn't speak of them until we went for tea to Ashton House.'

'When you pretended to have a headache?' Fanny said.

'I could scarcely believe that he returned my

96

feelings,' Esther said, 'and when he told me you were not averse to Henry's attentions then I hardly knew how to contain myself. Lady Ashton would have suspected something from my face had I stayed longer.'

'You never spoke of it to me,' Fanny said.

'I was waiting for you to say something first,' Esther explained. 'It would not have done, I suppose, to share confidences before Mother had been approached. You always knew the right way in which to behave, Fanny.'

'Yes. I suppose that's so,' Fanny said. She spoke as carefully and thoughtfully as if she were considering someone else.

'Now that Mother knows,' Esther said, 'there will be no harm in mentioning it among ourselves. Philip and Henry will speak to their parents very soon. Sir John will make no objection but Lady Ashton may be harder to win over. She was always more ambitious for her sons. You know Philip has such high regard for you, Fanny. I don't think he would have proposed at all if you had shown any signs of disliking the match!'

Fanny felt cold and sick listening to her sister rattle on happily, while all her own recent misconceptions unravelled before her. Philip had not been speaking of his affection for her but for Esther when they had strolled in the rose garden. What she had taken to be kindness towards her shy twin had been partiality, and the rose he had picked for her

97

had no deeper meaning than a gallant social gesture. She had misunderstood everything he had said to her and what she had taken to be a declaration of his passion had been an enquiry on his brother's behalf.

'I will need your advice if I'm to be mistress of Ashton House one day,' Esther was saying. 'I never could keep house properly and Ashton House is a very grand establishment.'

Esther living in the luxury of Ashton House. Esther driving down to the village in the Ashton carriage, with Philip's ring on her finger. Esther coming over to visit her sister, the curate's wife. Something in Fanny cooled and hardened and her thumping heart no longer raced. She had come within an ace of making a complete fool of herself. She glanced from below lowered lashes at her sister's pale, shining face and soft ringlets. How in the wide world had she succeeded in attracting Philip Ashton's attention so quickly? For the first time Fanny fancied she detected a certain shyness in her twin's expression. All Esther's fluttering ways, her dreaming looks and lilting voice, even her acts of absent-minded charity, appeared as bait to trap the most eligible young man in the district.

'I think,' she said slowly, 'that we ought to keep the news to ourselves for a while. It would be dreadful if wind of it blew to Sir John and Lady Ashton before Philip and Henry spoke to them. Oh, I know they are of full age and not bound to seek approval for their marriages but one would prefer to start right.'

'Oh, it would be dreadful to begin thus,' Esther agreed.

'So we'll say nothing for a few days. That will give us time to be sure.'

'Of our feelings?' Esther eyes widened. 'But I just couldn't be more certain of mine. When Philip first came into the room—oh, he was so much more handsome than I remembered, and then he took my hand and said, 'Come and dance with me, Esther,' as simply as that. And before the dance was done we could not look away from each other. Philip himself found it hard to believe. He thinks it a great jest that he and Henry should travel all over Europe and then fall in love with two local girls whom they've known since childhood.'

'A great jest,' Fanny said. Her heart was a cold lump of lead and it had never been harder to smile.

'If only there were three Ashton sons then Gobnait might be matched up too,' Esther remarked with a touch of wistfulness.

Henry had enquired about Gobnait first, Fanny remembered. She herself had been his second choice and Philip had never thought of her as a wife at all. She pressed her hands so tightly together that the knuckles showed white and said lightly, 'Gobnait will marry Edward Grant in the end, I daresay. We shall have to wait and see. Have you told her yet?'

'About Philip and myself?' Esther shook her head. 'I can't really believe that it's true! Anyway, I've hardly seen her since the uncles came. She can think of nothing but horses at the moment.'

'When did she ever think of anything else?' Fanny said, rising and holding out her hand to help the other to her feet. 'Our news will wait until we have the Ashtons' approval.'

'If you think so.' Esther, obedient as ever, spoke meekly. 'But I am so pleased for us both, Fanny! Shall we have a double wedding, do you think?'

'Time enough to talk about that later.' Fanny smiled, unable to bear any more. 'We'd better hurry. I've promised Catherine to alter a gown of mine for her wearing.'

'Do you think we should tell Catherine?' Esther asked.

'She has no suitors yet,' Fanny reminded her. 'It might make her feel slightly left out if she learned that two of us were betrothed. You'd not want to be unkind?'

'No, of course not. Poor Catherine! We must try to find a pleasant young man for her,' Esther said earnestly.

There was, thought Fanny, a bare possibility that Esther might have been mistaken, that Henry Ashton had actually offered for her. It was a hope that died as they entered the house and Fausty greeted them with a whispered, 'We'll keep this to ourselves until the news is

100

formally announced. Fanny, you must try not to fret about Henry. 'Tis only a summer cold.'

Fanny, going upstairs to change, wished savagely that it was plague. She craved privacy in order to go over in her mind recent conversations that she must have completely misinterpreted, in order to weep a little at this blow to all her hopes and dreams. Privacy was denied her. Catherine, all eager gratitude, was waiting for the dress to be altered and Fanny had to endure the tedium of taking in tucks and responding to her cousin's chatter.

'Surely some young gentleman will offer for me when he sees me looking like a grand lady in a fine dress! Not that I've much of a dowry, but I've linen sewn, and a shawl knitted, and my dada has promised me the price of a new pony if anyone takes me as a wife.'

'Someone is bound to notice you,' Fanny said mechanically.

'At the party? Is this the kind of dress an English young lady would be wearing to a party now?'

Fanny had forgotten about the suggested party. The thought of having an announcement made on such an occasion, of watching Esther with Philip at her side, was too much to bear. Hastily she said, 'It is too soon to have a party here yet. There is the York Show to come very soon when we meet all our neighbours. You will be introduced to a great many people then.'

By the time the altered dress was pronounced suitable Fanny's desire to weep had fled. Her eyes were dry and burning, her face stiff with the effort she had made to hide her feelings, but she was entirely in command of herself, so much so that she was able to sit chatting with the others in the drawing-room without any sense of strain. At least word of the betrothals had not reached the others. Fanny could not have endured the questions and comments of Patrick and the uncles. For a change they had rejected the tavern in favour of an evening at home and sat around the fire that Fausty had ordered to be lit, discussing the forthcoming show and Gobnait's chance of winning a prize.

'If she doesn't pull off the first prize then it will only be because I won it instead,' Patrick declared.

'And why shouldn't you indeed, with the pair of you half-Irish and created to sit in a saddle?' Stevie enquired rhetorically.

Fausty, sipping sherry, glanced at the elder twins with affectionate pride. Her brother was right. Patrick and Gobnait with their long, lean frames, bright hair surmounting narrow faces and high-bridged noses resembled elegant thoroughbreds. Patrick's laziness vanished like snow in summer when anyone put him near a hunting-field and Gobnait was all nervous, quicksilver energy.

Her glance shifted to Esther who sat, only

half-listening to the conversation. Her youngest daughter often had an air of listening to melodies unheard. She was too gentle for her own good, sometimes. Fausty hoped that Philip Ashton would prove a kindly husband and stand between Esther and his formidable mother, but his reluctance to tell his parents about his affection troubled her.

Fausty's brown eyes moved to where Fanny sat and a slight frown rose at the back of them. Fanny was the cleverest and the prettiest of them and would make a perfect wife for almost any man. Yet she had accepted Henry who was a pleasant enough young man but lacked his brother's looks or elegance. Had it been left to Fausty she would have matched Fanny with Philip. The frown changed to a rueful smile as she reminded herself that she had never been very perceptive about people. No doubt Fanny had seen qualities in Henry that others missed.

'The Ashtons have invited us to share luncheon with them on the day of the Show,' she said aloud. 'Philip told me this afternoon when he called.'

'To be sharing a box with lords and ladies now!' Sean exclaimed, nudging his brother. 'That'll be a fine tale to be telling when we get home.'

'You're not thinking of leaving us yet?' Fausty asked quickly. 'Why, you've scarcely arrived!'

If only they would leave, Fanny thought longingly. Their presence irritated her beyond bearing. They trampled mud into the clean house, they smoked incessantly, filling the air with clouds of blue-grey smoke, they sprawled on the sofa with their legs stretched out and told Irish jests. They lowered the tone of any company into which they came and the thought of having to introduce them to Lady Ashton made her flinch.

'We cannot detain them for ever,' she said aloud.

'Oh, I reckon we can stay until after Christmas,' Sean said, glinting a smile towards her. 'We've our niece to settle into a proposal before we think of leaving and twenty years conversation with Fausty to catch up with!'

His wide grin mocked her. Fanny was sure that he was aware of her disapproval and enjoyed discomposing her. Meeting his smile with a faint one of her own she said, 'Of course you are all most welcome to spend Christmas with us, Uncle Sean. The trouble is that we are frequently snowed in for weeks at a time and you would find us very dull.'

'Speak for yourself,' Patrick said, rising to refill his glass. 'Cousin Catherine, you must allow me to draw up a list of eligible gentlemen who may take your fancy. There are no dukes in the neighbourhood but I met a marquis two years ago.'

'All Catherine wants is a decent young man

104

willing to marry her and give her ten thousand pounds a year,' Stevie said, and winked.

Fanny rose abruptly, her face aching with the effort of holding her smile.

'I've a busy day tomorrow, so you'll excuse me if I retire now,' she said.

'The trouble with Fanny,' Patrick remarked as she left the room, 'is that she has no sense of humour.'

'Try believing yourself to be loved by someone who wants to marry your sister,' Fanny thought savagely, 'and then find out how much humour you can produce.'

There was no way of dislodging the uncles until after Christmas. That much was clear. She heaved a sigh, brushing them from her mind, and went slowly upstairs, not to sleep, but to sit in the gathering darkness, her chin on her clenched fist, and work out slowly and in great detail a plan that would avert the disaster looming over her.

'I think I will drive over to the Ashtons' and find out if Henry is recovering,' she announced after breakfast the next morning.

She had timed her remark carefully. The clear sunshine of the previous day had given place to an overcast sky, heavy with rain clouds. Gobnait and Patrick, being careless of weather, had ridden over to Otley with the uncles, and Esther, who hated damp as much as any cat, had gone upstairs with Catherine to sort out her trinket drawer.

'Give him our love,' Fausty said promptly. She would have liked to add a word of warning about not giving Lady Ashton cause to wonder at the unexpected visit, but Fanny was not one to accept advice patiently so she held her tongue, merely murmuring that it would be wise to take an umbrella. Privately she wondered if Fanny had also caught a chill. Her colour was unusually high and there were shadows under blue eyes.

It would have been a relief to be out of the house and bowling at a spanking pace across the moor had she not been going to Ashton House, but Fanny's mind was firmly set on two matters. Esther must not be permitted to marry Philip and she herself somehow or other must wriggle out of the engagement to Henry. Both marriages were sure to prove unhappy and, by preventing them, she was avoiding much future misery for all of them. Yet despite her resolution she felt a tremor of nervousness as she turned in at the open gates of Ashton House. She had rehearsed the dialogue in her own mind but everything depended on the other making the right responses.

Fortune was with her. There was no sign of the Ashton gentlemen but the butler, looking down his nose, informed her that Milady was 'At Home'.

Lady Ashton was in the large drawing-room and Fanny felt a pang when she entered. It was in this chamber that the tea party had been held; through these same long windows that she had stepped out into the rose garden. The windows were closed now and the grass beyond had a greyish tinge. Her hostess, not troubling to rise, greeted her with such a cool nod that Fanny would have suspected she guessed the state of affairs had the girl not been aware that she greeted everybody with the same frigidity.

She took the chair indicated and launched at once into her prepared speech.

'It is most good of you to see me, Lady Ashton. Certainly I hope not to take up too much of your time, but I am anxious to seek your advice.'

'And I shall be most happy to give it,' Lady Ashton said, unbending perceptibly.

'It is not a matter I feel able to discuss with my mother,' Fanny said, looking at her hands.

'You will take a glass of wine and a biscuit,' Lady Ashton said, giving the girl a sharp look and ringing a small handbell.

Fanny, on the verge of what seemed like a precipice, had begun to shake despite her resolution. What she was going to do was a terrible thing. She was too honest not to understand that the time might come when she would hate herself for setting in motion this train of events, but something dark and resentful drove her on.

A maidservant brought in the refreshments. The wine steadied her a little. She sipped it gratefully, then drew a deep breath.

'I am somewhat concerned about my sister,' she said at last.

'Which one? You have two, I believe?'

'My twin, Esther. She is my younger sister,' Fanny explained.

'A pale, quiet girl. I thought her very ladylike and sweet-tempered.'

'Oh, she is,' Fanny exclaimed. 'She is the best natured creature in the world. What troubles me is—' She hesitated, still poised on the brink of the precipice. There was still time to draw back, to say something less damaging.

'I have other visitors coming,' Lady Ashton hinted, glancing at the handsome ormolu clock on the mantelshelf.

Fanny drew another deep breath and leaped.

'Esther is not strong,' she said. 'I do not mean merely that she is delicate, though she is that too. She is—absent-minded. Whole days will pass while she wanders about quite indifferent to what's going on around her. She is not able to cope with life at all.'

'What exactly are you trying to say?' Lady Ashton enquired.

The woman had spoken the very line that Fanny had imagined for her.

'I don't like to ask my mother,' she said, 'but my father's maiden aunts, Sassie and Dorothy Sabre—Sassie was killed in the barn blaze but Aunt Dotty died when we were small. I remember her as always very kind and— absent-minded?'

'Weak in the head,' Lady Ashton pronounced. 'Everybody in the neighbourhood knew that Dotty Sabre was weak in the head.'

'Mother would never have it so,' Fanny confessed, 'but I do sometimes worry lest Esther takes after Aunt Dotty. I worry lest her dreaminess conceals something more.'

'This is a family matter on which I am scarcely qualified to pronounce,' Lady Ashton said, and promptly proceeded to do so. 'My own opinion is based merely upon what I remember of Dotty Sabre. She was my senior by many years and we saw very little of her, but she was decidedly odd. I believe she had been odd since childhood, though she was never in the least dangerous.'

'Oh, I didn't mean to suggest—' Fanny began, and was silenced by the wave of a hand.

'I believe that in many families, especially where there are twins, one child may prove slower, more eccentric than the others,' Lady Ashton continued. 'I do wonder if the amount of intelligence available for the offspring of two people is not circumscribed by Nature. One often finds idiocy in a large family—not that I am suggesting that applies to your sister, my dear. It seems to me, from what you have said, that confined within the bosom of her family in a placid environment she will remain quite happy and secure. Girls with delicate nerves should be gently treated.'

'She is my twin, you see, and I do feel somewhat responsible for her,' Fanny put in.

'Your brother and sister should take some share of the responsibility,' Lady Ashton said.

'Oh, I do beg you to say nothing,' Fanny said in alarm. 'Patrick and Gobnait have their own lives to lead, but Esther and I have always been very close.'

'Oh, I assure you that I shall keep our talk in the strictest confidence,' the other said quickly. 'My view is you have very little to worry about. Esther is a dear, sweet girl and I am sure she is fortunate to have a sister who is so mindful of her well-being.'

'I find that life is very hard sometimes,' Fanny said, 'as I grow older.'

'You are very young still.' Lady Ashton gave her a sympathetic look. 'In my opinion it is not a good thing to force too much responsibility onto a young girl's shoulders. Your brother should take his share of the running of your household instead of wasting his time in carousing. I hear that you have begun to take the fleeces to market.'

'We hope to increase the profits this year,' Fanny said. 'There are four of us to keep, and now my mother's Irish relatives have come to stay.'

'I heard,' Lady Ashton said, a wealth of meaning in the two words.

'So you do understand that I must make

110

certain that Esther is always cared for,' Fanny said.

'I understand that you were quite right to confide in me,' Lady Ashton said. 'If you are troubled about anything in the future you must come to me. I pride myself on having some experience of human nature.'

She bowed gravely and rang the handbell again. It was her signal for the butler to hover in the doorway. Fanny rose. Her trembling had ceased and she had not yet begun to hate herself. What had been planted in Lady Ashton's mind would take strong root and then choke any notion of a marriage between Philip and Esther.

'I trust Henry is better? We heard that he was indisposed,' she said.

'A mere cold.' His mother shrugged an elegant shoulder. 'Gentlemen always make such a fuss over trifles.'

'There was another matter.' Fanny glanced at the butler who discreetly withdrew.

'I am expecting visitors,' Lady Ashton repeated. Her barely-concealed impatience hinted that her stock of neighbourly concern was running low.

'It is merely about the Horse Show at York,' Fanny said. 'Sir John was kind enough to offer us places in your box there, but as we have visitors it will be too many. My mother is sure you won't take offence.'

'Not at all.' Lady Ashton positively beamed.

'I hope you have a pleasant day there.'

'As long as Esther doesn't find the excitement too much for her,' Fanny murmured as she made her curtsy.

To say more would have been to gild the lily. She curtsied again and left the room, stepping lightly and briskly after the butler's ponderous frame. Philip was coming up the drive as she climbed up into the trap and, for a moment she felt a clutch at her heart that was as bad as physical pain. If Esther had not employed her sly, conniving ways to entrap him Philip would have fallen in love with her and she would never have needed to make this visit.

'Fanny, how pleasant to see you!' Dismounting, he came to the side of the trap and smiled at her. 'Nothing is wrong, I hope?'

'Nothing at all. I merely came to enquire after Henry's health.'

'Oh, he will be up and about in a few days,' he said easily.

'You have not spoken to your parents?'

'No,' he hesitated slightly. 'The truth is I'm reluctant to spring this on my mother without warning. Henry and I agreed it would be better to wait until after the Show. As we are spending the day together then she will have the opportunity of getting to know both of you more intimately. By then she will realize that something is in the wind.'

The truth, Fanny thought, was that he and

112

his brother were as nervous of Lady Ashton as everybody else was. Such weakness in a handsome young man in no way disappointed her. It gave her a pleasantly protective feeling towards him.

'My mother thinks it would be better if we had separate boxes at the Show,' she said. 'We will be such a crowd with the Irish relatives that nobody would be comfortable.'

'Well, at least we can spend part of the day together,' he said. 'I expect Gobnait will win the red rosette. She has a new mount she was telling me about.'

'Gobnait is a wonderful rider,' Fanny agreed with enthusiasm. 'It is such a pity that Esther fears horses.'

'She's a very sensitive girl,' Philip said. He spoke so tenderly that Fanny made an involuntary movement of protest.

'You mustn't fret about Henry.' Philip had misinterpreted and gave her a look of sympathy. 'It really is nothing serious.'

'It is not that.' She returned his look with an appealing one of her own. 'I was just thinking that I ought to feel more concern. If Henry and I are truly suited then I would be most concerned over his indisposition but I feel only as I might feel about a friend.'

'You and Henry must spend more time together,' Philip advised. 'He's shy, you know, a bit awkward with the ladies. He needs a vigorous, jolly girl like you to bring him out.

Depend upon it but he improves on acquaintance.'

'Vigorous and jolly'! Rage brought colour into Fanny's face and a sparkle to her blue eyes. Meekly she said. 'I am sure that you are right, but we live so quietly here and recent events seem to have whirled us along so fast that we have scarcely had time to think!'

'Esther has no misgivings, has she?' He looked faintly alarmed.

'Oh, no.' Fanny shook her head, smiling. 'Dear Esther is quite heedless. She will rush towards every new experience without the smallest thought. In many ways she is so like a child that I tremble for her. I am only thankful that it was yourself who first offered for her, otherwise she might have accepted the first man who came along.'

Out of the corner of her eye she could discern an edge of curtain at one of the windows being lifted. It would certainly not be wise to have Lady Ashton begin to wonder at the length and intimacy of the conversation.

Steeling her heart against the trouble that clouded Philip's dark eyes, she said briskly as she took up the reins, 'I expect I am fretting about nothing and Henry and I will match very well together. Good-day to you, Philip. I will tell Esther that you send love.'

CHAPTER SEVEN

Events, Fanny decided, were turning out to her advantage. The recent fine weather had given place to a steady downpour which kept all but the hardiest indoors and raised grave doubts about whether the Horse Show would be successful.

'The turf will be too soft for the mare,' Gobnait said, chewing her lower lip in vexation.

'The rain will clear.' Fausty, who was always inclined to optimism, glanced through the window at the teeming sky.

'If this were Ireland now it would be a different tale,' Sean said. 'Do you remember the Dublin rain, Fausty?'

'That I do.' Her brown eyes misted slightly. 'Soft as wishes and clean as virtue, and seemingly to last for eternity!'

'The rain in Yorkshire has more sense,' Fanny said briskly, hoping to forestall a bout of nostalgia. 'It always clears up in time for the Show.'

'I wish we were going into the box with the grand ladies and gentlemen,' Catherine said wistfully.

'Lady Ashton feared that we might all be a trifle cramped,' Fanny said.

'If we'd been earls,' Stevie remarked, 'the

lady wouldn't have thought twice about the cramping! We'll not be taking any notice of the snub, Catherine darling. We'll rise above it.'

'Don't you mean "float"?' Fanny interposed, darting a look at the tumbler of whisky in his hand.

'Oh, oh, but we're out of favour.' He rose, grinning at her in the impudent fashion that set her teeth on edge. 'Sean, shall we go and join Patrick in the stables? We can make private wagers on whether the Show's to be held or not.'

He lounged out, followed by his twin. Catherine, looking unhappy, trailed after them.

'That wasn't very kind, Fanny dear,' Fausty said in gentle reproof. 'You will make them feel unwelcome.'

'That would take more than me to achieve,' Fanny said. 'I'm sorry, Mother. I don't mean to be unkind but honestly! This visit has been going on for ever and they do nothing but sit around the house and the stables, drinking the last of Father's whisky and making the most terrible jokes.'

'I think the uncles are fun,' Gobnait said defiantly, whisking out. 'I shall go and join them and talk horses!'

'They'll encourage her too!' Fanny said crossly. 'Mother, Gobnait will never get Edward Grant to propose if she spends all her waking hours in the saddle. You really ought to

116

speak to her.'

'Let me get you and Esther up the aisle first,' Fausty protested.

'Hush! One of the others may hear,' Fanny warned.

'And that's something that troubles *me*!' Fausty had lowered her voice but her tone was agitated. 'Why must there be all this secrecy? It's as if Philip and Henry were ashamed of wanting to marry you both.'

'They don't wish to make it public until they've talked to Sir John and Lady Ashton,' Fanny said.

'Patrick and Gobnait are hardly members of the public,' Fausty objected. 'We have never kept secrets from one another in this family. How long are we supposed to wait before the public announcement is made, and what happens if Lady Ashton doesn't approve? She has not displayed any great partiality for us so far.'

'Nor is she likely to,' Fanny argued, 'if we thrust our Irish relatives under her nose. She is very much a lady, Mother, and we ought not to blame her for that.'

'I'm not ashamed of my relatives,' Fausty said, her colour deepening.

'Of course not,' Fanny agreed. 'I am merely trying to explain how Lady Ashton might look at the matter. Of course Philip and Henry may wed where they choose but it will be so much more comfortable if they have parental

117

approval.'

'It is not as if they have courted you for a long time.' Fausty was launched on her own train of thought. 'Why, they were scarcely arrived home again before they offered for you.'

'Surely you're not complaining because two handsome gentlemen have fallen in love with us?' Fanny said, laughing.

'If they're so much in love,' her mother said testily, 'they should be visiting more often. We've not seen either of them for days!'

'Henry has been indisposed,' Fanny excused, 'and the weather is bad.'

'Henry is surely recovered by now, and it would take more than a drop of rain to keep a proper man from his courting,' Fausty argued.

'Nor a Yorkshireman.' Fanny who was nearer the window had spotted a figure riding across the wet grass. 'Will you excuse me if I go and receive Henry?'

'I'll keep the others out of the way,' Fausty said, beaming.

By the time Fanny reached the door Huldah was admitting the visitor, her voice raised in scolding.

'Just up from a sick-bed and out in this downpour! You should have better sense, sir! Let me have your hat and cloak for 'tis dripping wet.'

'Huldah, bring some hot toddy into the small parlour,' Fanny interrupted. 'Good-day,

Henry, won't you come to the fire? Mother sends her apologies but she's up to her eyes in household duties!'

She led the way into the small parlour, holding herself erect to disguise the faint tremor of nervousness that shook her. There was something in Henry's unsmiling countenance that made her suspect this was more than a social call.

'No refreshments, Huldah.' He paused briefly before following.

'Oh, but surely you'll take something?' Fanny turned as he closed the door.

'Nothing, thank you. I really cannot stay for more than a few minutes.'

'Something is wrong?' She seated herself by the fire and looked up at him anxiously.

'I have grave news.' He hesitated, then said in a rush, 'My parents have refused their consent to Philip's marriage.'

'What?' She looked at him blankly. The news was hardly surprising but she had not expected Henry to bring it.

'We both spoke to my parents,' he said. Father was quite happy to agree but my mother, while grudgingly agreeing to our marriage, utterly refused to consider any prospect of a union between Philip and your sister.'

'For what reason?' Now was the moment to put indignation into her tone, but to her surprise she felt genuine anger.

'She gave no reason save that she would not agree. She declared that if Philip persisted in his determination then she would see to it that he was disinherited—actually disinherited!'

'And she gave no reason?'

'None to me. She talked to father privately though and, after that, he joined his voice to hers. Philip will lose the estate if he goes through with this marriage. They are both adamant.'

'What objection could they possibly have to Esther?' Fanny demanded.

'My mother refuses to say anything and my father speaks only of delicate health being a bar.'

'Then they give credence to the old rumour,' Fanny said.

'What old rumour?' He was staring at her.

'You have surely heard of it?' she said in a low rapid voice. 'My late father had two unmarried aunts.'

'Miss Sassie and Miss Dorothy,' he nodded.

'Aunt Sassie and my father died when he was trying to rescue her from a blazing barn. That was just before Esther and I were born. Aunt Dotty—did you truly never hear the rumour?'

'No.' He frowned in bewilderment.

'My mother has absolutely forbidden any of us to speak about it,' Fanny said sadly. 'There was a tale that the fire in the barn wasn't an accident, that Aunt Dotty—she was always a trifle peculiar. I can recall her when I was small, wandering about and singing to herself. She never went out anywhere and she sometimes forgot our names.'

'And Esther is like that? Surely not!'

'I don't like to think so either,' Fanny hastened to say, 'but there is no denying that Esther is terribly absent-minded. We who love her are accustomed to her little ways but if she begins to go out and about in society there might be comment from those who are less favourably inclined towards her. Oh, Henry, I hoped for so much from this marriage! Your brother is so strong, so protective, that with his support her condition might have remained stable, even improved.'

'Philip doesn't know. I'll swear that Philip doesn't know,' Henry said in agitation.

'Then it might be kinder not to tell him,' she murmured.

'And leave him in ignorance of the true reason behind our mother's prohibition?'

'I cannot believe a marriage would be too harmful,' Fanny said gently. 'Oh, there may be some risk concerning the children born of such a marriage, but I cannot pretend to any medical knowledge about such matters.'

'My mother was adamant,' he repeated unhappily.

'Perhaps she has some further knowledge,' Fanny said. 'I cannot believe that Lady Ashton would stand in the way of Philip's and Esther's happiness unless she felt that she had good reason.'

'My parents are most concerned about our happiness,' he said earnestly, 'but marriage is a solemn undertaking and cannot depend entirely on romantic considerations. Philip will inherit the property so it is most important that he choose the right wife.'

'You put it so clearly,' Fanny said, wondering why she had never realized until this moment how incredibly pompous he was. She could imagine him in ten or fifteen years time, thicker about the waist, his voice more sonorous as he lectured his parishioners on the virtues of frugality after he had enjoyed a luncheon of roast pheasant washed down with claret.

'This is a sad state of affairs,' he pronounced gloomily.

'Sad indeed.' She looked up at him, making her eyes soft. 'You realize that this makes our union impossible?'

'My mother has not withheld her consent.'

'But how could I agree to become your wife when my own sister is prevented from wedding the man of her choice?' Fanny questioned sadly. 'We are twins after all.'

'I am sure there is no weakness of intellect in you,' Henry protested.

'I confess I am aware of none,' she admitted, 'unless it has not yet begun to develop. But if Esther is not to receive the

122

support of a husband I cannot cause her further pain by depriving her of the company of a sister.'

'We could both help her in every possible way,' he argued.

'I am not only thinking of Esther,' she said impatiently. 'Do you think that I have no feelings? Do you think I could bear to be married into a family who had rejected my sister, even if their rejection was based on sound reasoning? Henry, forgive me but it would be better if we agreed to remain friendly but put out of our minds any notion of marrying.'

'This is a very heavy blow,' he said morosely.

'But not too heavy,' she said shrewdly. 'Come, it was Gobnait who first caught your eye until you learned she was keeping company with Edward Grant. Why, you never even proposed to me yourself but left it to Philip to enquire on your behalf. You are not so much in love with me that a refusal will cast you down!'

'I shall have to make my way in the clerical profession, so I naturally require a suitable helpmate,' he said, looking faintly discomposed.

'There you are then.' She reached to pat his arm. 'I cannot see myself being any kind of help to a rising young clergyman when I would be forever fretting about Esther.'

'It is still a heavy blow,' he said.

'But one from which you will recover,' Fanny said. 'Though Esther will be heart-broken. She has always taken everything so much to heart. Even the smallest thing will cast her down for weeks.'

'I shall have to see her,' he said.

'You mean Philip will not be giving her the bad news himself?' Fanny asked.

'He flung out of the house in a towering rage,' Henry said. 'I feared he might be coming straight here but I expect he has gone to drown his sorrows in the tavern.'

A doubt flickered at the edge of Fanny's mind. A young man disappointed in love who rushed off to get intoxicated had a decidedly weak side to his character. For an instant she wondered if such a man would prove a suitable husband. Then there rushed over her the memory of dark eyes and a charming smile and the doubt was crushed down. Whatever weakness lay in Philip could be overcome by a vigorous young wife. It was all the more reason why she, not Esther, was better fitted to be his bride.

'It would be wiser for me to break the news to her,' she said slowly. 'I cannot begin to tell you how much I fear the effect this will have on her. She is most distressingly sensitive.'

'What can you possibly say to mitigate the shock?' His face was full of honest concern.

'You must leave that to me,' Fanny said with decision. 'I will put it in the kindest way I can but it will be very hard. At least try to prevent Philip from coming here. It would upset her dreadfully to have to receive him when their union has been forbidden.'

'And you will not reconsider our own case?' He was looking at her hopefully but she could sense the relief in him when she answered.

'It would be quite impossible, my dear. Let us agree to remain friends. Leave now and trust me to break the news to Esther and to mother without saying too much to disturb them. Tell Philip how deeply grieved I am, but I'm certain your parents act from the best possible motives.'

He pressed her hands and went somewhat ponderously from the room. Fanny sank down into the fireside chair and wrapped her arms around herself in an effort to contain the fit of nervous trembling that gripped her. So far it had all gone according to the plan she had formed. Lady Ashton had forbidden the match and she herself had wriggled out of an engagement to Henry. There was little possibility of Philip's defying the prohibition. He would never risk being disinherited.

'Fanny, has something happened?' Esther asked, hurrying into the room. 'I met Henry on his way out and when I greeted him he mumbled something about being terribly sorry and almost ran through the door! There is nothing wrong with Philip, is there? I've not seen him since he called here and asked for mother's permission for us to wed. He's not taken Henry's cold, has he?'

'Philip is perfectly well,' Fanny said quickly. 'Come and sit down, Esther. There is something we must discuss.'

'Then something is wrong.' Esther, who for all her vagueness, could be sharply intuitive, looked at her.

'Henry came to tell us that he and Philip had spoken to their parents,' Fanny began.

'And Lady Ashton made objection! I knew that she would not consider us half good enough for her sons,' Esther interrupted, her pale eyes filling with tears. 'I warned Philip that she might be difficult but he assured me she thought me a very ladylike young person.'

'Which is not the same as saying she would welcome either of us as a daughter-in-law,' Fanny said.

'She *has* voiced objections then?' Esther attempted a somewhat woebegone smile and straightened her narrow shoulders in expectation of a blow.

'My dear sister, she has utterly refused to countenance any such notion,' Fanny said.

'Then Philip has a hard task to talk her round,' Esther said.

'Philip has an impossible task,' Fanny corrected. 'Both she and Sir John declare that Philip will lose his inheritance if he persists in wanting to marry you. They will take no argument or persuasion.'

'And Henry came to break the news? Surely Philip will come himself?'

'And risk his entire future? Lady Ashton has forbidden any further communication between you.'

'But she must have some serious reason to ruin our happiness so,' Esther said. 'We expected opposition but not a cold refusal!'

'Philip has acceded to her wish,' Fanny said.

'But he loves me. He would never give me up so easily.'

'He is to be owner of Ashton House and heir to a considerable fortune,' Fanny said. 'It's a harsh fact to face but it would take a very great love to weigh in the scales against that.'

'But he did love me. He does love me,' Esther gulped.

'I am sure he made you believe so,' Fanny said gently. 'For my own part I was certain that Henry had fallen in love with me. But the feeling cannot have been as deep or lasting as we thought. Perhaps it's for the best.'

'I don't see how it can possibly be.' Esther choked back a sob.

'Oh, my dear, what kind of man sets aside his affection for a girl merely on the whim of his mother?' Fanny protested.

'But if he is to be disinherited—oh, I cannot believe that Lady Ashton could be so cruel!'

'The estate is a considerable one. Philip is not trained for any profession save that of squire,' Fanny pointed out. 'It would mean his losing everything.'

'To Henry. Oh, Fanny, that might not be so bad,' Esther said eagerly. 'You would make a much better mistress of Ashton House than I would. I never know the right thing to say in company!'

'Esther, you cannot mean to be so selfish!' Fanny exclaimed. 'The last thing in the world Henry wants is to be saddled with the management of Ashton House when he has his heart set on a bishopric.'

'I didn't know,' Esther said blankly.

'Not that I shall marry Henry now of course.' Fanny leaned forward, clasping her sister's hands tightly. 'No, it is not merely out of pique because of Philip's jilting you, though it has certainly influenced my decision. I have felt for some time that I don't feel towards him as a girl ought to feel towards the man she intends to marry. And Lady Ashton has made it clear that her consent was given most grudgingly. The truth is that she does not consider either of us good enough for her precious sons.'

'But Philip has not even come himself to tell me.' Esther pulled her hands away and rose, walking in agitation up and down the room, her voice shaking as she declared, 'He cannot be so cruel as to send such a message by his brother! I must go to Ashton House and demand an explanation. That is the least he owes me after all the promises he made!'

'My dear, that would be the worst thing you could possibly do!' Fanny had paled slightly. 'Why, he would have no respect for you at all if you were to do such a thing. It would merely serve to prove to Lady Ashton that you had not been properly reared, and one could scarcely blame her. It would reflect great discredit on our poor mother.'

'I had forgotten Mother.' Esther put her hands to her cheeks in dismay. 'She will fly into the worst temper when she knows what has happened. I wouldn't put it past her to ride over to Ashton House and belabour Lady Ashton over the head with an umbrella!'

'I wouldn't put it past her either,' Fanny said gloomily. 'Esther, you cannot allow Mother to guess how deeply you feel about him. Make her believe that your affections are not so deeply engaged that this will ruin your whole life! It will be necessary for both of us to hide our real hurt. There is one blessing at least! No announcement has been made, even in the family.'

'But Gobnait and Patrick must have a notion of something in the wind,' Esther interrupted. 'I told Gobnait that something exciting might happen soon.'

'If Patrick were to discover that we had been jilted,' Fanny said, 'he'd likely call Philip out. Duelling is against the law so one might end up in prison and the other—the other might be killed!'

'I shall tell them that I have altered my mind,' Esther said. She spoke with a kind of sad dignity, wiping her eyes on a scrap of lace-edged linen drawn from her sleeve.

'Perhaps they won't ask.' Fanny wiped her own eyes, summoning a smile as she rose. 'We will keep this to ourselves. By the time the Horse Show comes—'

'I'll not go to it,' Esther said. 'I couldn't bear to be in—in company. I truly couldn't bear it, Fanny.'

'We'll decide later. Perhaps you'll alter your mind by then,' Fanny said comfortingly.

'I shall never alter my mind about Philip,' Esther said in a small, tight voice. 'I love him, Fanny. I shall always love him even though he hasn't been near me himself to tell me of Lady Ashton's prohibition. I shall never change, Fanny, and I shall never love anyone else.'

Her voice broke on the last word and she hurried from the room without looking back.

Fanny wrung her hands together in an effort to warm them. She felt cold all through and her legs were shaking. It had been much more painful than she had dreamed. The look in her sister's eyes had reminded her too strongly of a dog that had been caught in a gin-trap near the mill. She and Patrick had come across it during a stroll and Patrick had shot it. In a way, she told herself, she was only doing what her brother had been forced to do. Esther would have been miserable wed to Philip. He needed

130

a bright, forceful girl to help him stand up for himself against his formidable mother. In time Esther would realize that it was all for the best. In time.

CHAPTER EIGHT

'What the devil ails Esther?' Patrick enquired lazily. 'I asked her what she intended to wear at the Show and she burst into tears and said she wasn't going.'

'She has a cold and has decided to stay at home,' Fanny said.

'A cold? I've seen no sign of it,' Patrick said.

'You're so often in the tavern that I'm surprised you ever notice anything,' she retorted.

'Glory be to God, but aren't you the saintly one!' Sean, lounging by the window, turned his head to grin at them.

'If you will excuse me, Uncle, I was talking to my brother,' Fanny said stiffly.

'Don't mind her. She always had too much dignity for her inches,' Patrick said. 'In my opinion there's been a falling out in the dovecot and Esther has taken a fit of the sulks. You know she's not the only one. Philip Ashton has ridden off to Hull and sends word that he won't be present either.'

He cocked an eyebrow at his sister who found herself flushing uncomfortably. Hastily she said, 'I believe Esther and Philip have had a—misunderstanding. People have begun to link their names in a manner embarrassing to both.'

'Why, I'd have sworn that Philip was as taken with her as Henry is with you,' Patrick began.

'Henry Ashton and me!' Fanny exclaimed, achieving an amused laugh. 'Well there you are, you see. A mild flirtation with a neighbour is worked up by the gossips into a full-blown engagement. It is nothing more than that.'

'Esther did seem upset,' he persisted.

'At missing the Show, I daresay.' Fanny, catching sight of her mother crossing the hall, whisked after her.

Fausty, looking less cheerful than usual, paused on the threshold of the dining-room and turned an anxious face.

'Fanny, can you tell me what is going on in this family?' she complained. 'First the Ashtons come to ask my consent to a couple of secret betrothals. Now Esther tells me that she and Philip have decided not to be married and you have decided not to wed Henry, and not a word more can I get out of anyone, for the Ashtons haven't been near and every time I see Esther she is in tears.'

'Esther is so tender-hearted she hates the thought of hurting anyone's feelings,' Fanny said.

'And there is no reason for her to miss the Show. This has not been, thank heaven, a public scandal,' Fausty continued.

'She has a cold.'

'Which doesn't surprise me in the least,'

Fausty said irritably, 'when she has spent hours wandering about on the wet moor. Oh, I know the rain has cleared but the grass is still wet. Yesterday she didn't return until dusk.'

'She wanted to be private, I suppose.'

'Surely this house is large enough to afford as much privacy as anybody could wish?' Fausty said.

'Not when we have so many visitors,' Fanny couldn't resist saying.

'My two brothers and my niece are scarcely a houseful,' her mother said defensively. 'Really, Fanny, you seem to be completely set against your relatives. I had hoped for a pleasant summer and you have done very little to bring it about.'

'Don't fret, Mother.' Fanny was moved to give her mother a rare hug. 'Catherine is perfectly sweet and I grow more and more fond of her, and I do try to put up with the uncles, honestly! We will have to leave Esther to work out her own affairs.'

'And you?' Fausty's brown eyes met the blue ones. 'Are you certain that you don't wish to marry Henry Ashton? He's a very worthy young man, with a living promised.'

'Worthy and dull,' Fanny said and looked for a moment like a younger, more mischievous, version of her mother. 'I never realized quite how pompous he had grown until I told him that I'd marry him. And when Esther confided to me her own doubts about

134

her union with Philip that made it easier for me to make up my mind and to end my own betrothal.'

'No doubt you know your own mind,' Fausty sighed.

'I think it would be most foolish to marry a man with whom one was not in love,' Fanny said. 'I want my marriage to be as perfect as yours. It was perfect, wasn't it?'

'I was in love with your father,' Fausty said. 'He was very handsome. The portrait never did him justice. But our marriage was very brief.'

'Was it happy enough?' For the first time there was a qualm of doubt in the girl's voice.

'Your father was a good man,' Fausty said. 'It was a tragedy that he died young when we had been wed such a short time.'

'And I shall marry someone exactly like him,' Fanny said. 'Or as much like him as possible. Henry is not the one. I'm thankful I found it out in time.'

'At least I am spared having Lady Ashton related to me by marriage,' Fausty said, regaining her good humour, 'but I am very fond of Philip. Such a charming young gentleman. It would have been nice to see Esther as mistress of Ashton House.'

'She would have been perfectly miserable,' Fanny said energetically. 'Philip is far too much under his mother's thumb to make the kind of strong husband that Esther needs. He requires a wife who would bring out his independence of mind and stand up with him against family pressure.'

'Perhaps you're right.' Fausty's brow wore a faint frown. It cleared as she shook her head slightly and said brightly, 'Well, it will all work out for the best, God willing!'

'Would you like me to stay at home with Esther when you go to the Show?' Fanny asked.

'No, there's no point in both of you missing the occasion,' Fausty said. 'Anyway, Esther may feel better by then. I cannot help being relieved that we are not to share the Ashton box. It would have been most awkward.'

'There is no reason why we should not remain friendly,' Fanny murmured. 'I intend to remain on cordial terms with both Henry and Philip. Mother, what are you going to wear? The black velvet is very handsome.'

'It make me look fifty,' Fausty said. 'Stevie was teasing me only the other day about the fact that I've worn black for nearly twenty years.'

'But you're in mourning. You're a widow.'

'Aye, so I am.' Fausty's lips curved into a faintly ironic smile. 'My heart is buried in your father's grave.'

'Are you joking?' Fanny enquired, puzzled.

'Yes, my pet. I'm joking.' Fausty gave her daughter a pat that had something of sadness about it and went out.

Fanny moved over to the fireplace and stood, gazing up at the portrait. Her father had been auburn-haired and grey-eyed, and Philip was dark, but she fancied there was a resemblance between them in the set of their mouths. Earl Sabre had been a popular and respected gentleman whose tragic death had plunged his widow into mourning for twenty years. That was the truth of it, she told herself.

'I will wear my blue dress,' she said aloud. The possibility that Philip might not go to the Show crossed her mind and was as swiftly dismissed. He would surely attend and then she would find the opportunity to let him know that she sympathized with his feelings. In time he would turn to her and realize that he needed not a sly, wishy washy creature but a young woman of spirit and courage.

'Did you say something?' Catherine enquired from the doorway.

'I was talking to my father.' Fanny indicated the portrait, adding softly, 'I wish I had known him.'

'Surely Patrick takes after him,' her cousin said.

'Patrick? Patrick is not in the least like father!' Fanny exclaimed.

'They both have red hair,' Catherine pointed out.

'Father's hair was a true auburn, and that's not important anyway,' Fanny said crossly. 'Earl Sabre was a fine, vigorous squire who died a hero's death. My brother boasts of being the laziest man in the entire county of Yorkshire. All he cares about is drinking and wenching.'

'I think Patrick is a beautiful young man,' Catherine said. There was a dreaminess in her eyes and voice that made the older girl look at her sharply.

'Patrick must learn to take care of his responsibilities,' she said warningly. 'The mill was left in trust for him but he never goes near. It sets a very bad example to the weavers for how can they be expected to take pride in what they do when the master never appears? However, none of that's your concern. You'll be going back to Ireland.'

'When I've caught a husband,' Catherine said and giggled. 'The uncles will be furious if I don't find a bridegroom, for they'll take it as a personal insult to the entire family.'

'We'll find you one at the Show. All the local farmers will be there with their sons,' Fanny said briskly, ignoring Catherine's doubtful expression. 'We shall make you look as pretty as a picture! You may keep the cloak I lent you and we'll sew new ribbons on the bonnet.'

Chattering, she put her arm about the other's waist and guided her from the room.

*   *   *

The landscape glinted with the rain that had fallen during the night when the day of the Horse Show dawned. Fanny, to her own surprise, had slept deeply and the face that greeted her in the mirror was vividly pretty.

'You look charming, Fanny Sabre,' she informed her reflection.

'Is that so?' Huldah, bringing in the hot water, set the jug down with a slight thump. 'If I were you, Miss, I'd wait until someone else said that to you.'

'Perhaps they will.' Fanny loosened her hair and ran her fingers through it.

'Not if you run around jilting perfectly decent young men,' Huldah said. 'No need to give me that injured look. I know most of what goes on in this family and what I don't know I shall find out.'

'You had better mind your own business, Huldah,' Fanny said coldly, her colour rising.

'With pleasure,' Huldah said equably. 'If you'll keep your nose out of other folks' affairs.'

She had plodded out before the girl could find any retort. Fanny glanced after her and then, catching her own expression in the glass, carefully rearranged her features into a smile. Today nothing would be allowed to disturb her calm and composed exterior.

She looked fully as charming as she believed when she was finally ready in the sable-banded cream cloak over the blue dress with its layers of lacy petticoats. The bonnet of pleated cream silk framed her small face and matched the slender umbrella that dangled from her wrist.

On the landing she hesitated, glancing uncertainly towards her sister's closed door. The least she could do was to look in and say something of comfort.

She tapped and entered the cluttered mess in the midst of which Esther sat. To Fanny's surprise her twin was neither drooping nor tearful. Her normally pale face was flushed and her lips were set in a tight line.

'You've developed a fever!' Exclaiming, Fanny crossed the room and took her sister's hand, feeling for the pulse. It beat rapidly but seemed regular enough.

'I was wondering whether or not to go after all,' Esther said.

'To the Show? Darling, is that wise? The Ashtons will be there and you don't want them to think you are forcing yourself on their notice, do you?' Fanny said earnestly.

'But there will be hundreds of people there,' Esther said. 'Why, we don't even have to meet the Ashtons unless we wish.'

'Of course, if you're sure it won't upset you.'

'Upset me *not* to see Lady Asthon?' Esther queried in surprise.

'I meant that if you cut her there will be a great deal of gossip and that would upset you very much,' Fanny said.

'Perhaps I had better stay at home then,' Esther waved her hands in a helpless fashion. 'Fanny, tell me what to do for Heaven's sake! I will follow your advice. Am I to go or stay?'

'For my own part I'd welcome your company,' Fanny said, 'but it would be grossly selfish of me solely to consider myself. You would be greatly unhappy if you came and found Philip not present, and equally miserable if he were there and didn't talk to you because of his mother's prohibition. You would not enjoy yourself.'

'You think I ought to stay at home then?'

'I think it would be foolish to expose yourself to needless misery,' Fanny said gently.

Esther drew a long breath and said. 'Then I will stay at home. I daresay it will be more sensible anyway as my cold has been truly bad.'

'You do look flushed.' Fanny spoke with heartfelt relief. The prospect of Philip and Esther contriving to meet at the Show on the very day they had planned to announce their betrothal dismayed her. More time must elapse before they could be allowed to meet. She herself needed more time.

'I think I'll go back to bed for a while,' Esther was saying. 'You will contrive to enjoy yourself, won't you? I shall want to know all about everything when you come home.'

'I promise.' Fanny bent and kissed the other's cheek. Esther's skin was dry and burning and there was a glitter in her eyes that

141

caused her sister a moment's alarm. Esther might deny it but she did seem feverish. The pleasure of the day ahead was clouded.

'Hurry or you'll be late. Catherine has already left,' Esther said.

'She can't have done. Mother isn't in the carriage yet.'

'She rode on ahead with Patrick,' Esther told her. 'The uncles are helping Gobnait get the new pony into the horse-box. You know I believe that Patrick admires Catherine very greatly. Do you think that something might come of it?'

'Patrick and Catherine? Don't be so ridiculous!' Fanny said curtly.

'I think Catherine is very pretty and very sweet.'

'And will make a very suitable wife for some farmer or merchant. She is scarcely fitted to be mistress of Sabre Hall. Don't fret if we're a little late. Huldah will be here and she'll send word if you feel worse.'

Fanny spoke with her usual calm common sense as she went out, but her own colour had risen. Esther was a romantic fool if she believed that Patrick would ever take a serious interest in Catherine. On the other hand there was no denying that the Irish girl had a certain appealing charm and Patrick might amuse himself with a flirtation. It would be better for everybody's peace of mind when Catherine was betrothed.

'Do hurry, dear.' Fausty, pulling on her gloves as she hurried across the hall, spoke impatiently. 'The others have all left. Is Esther all right? She seemed a mite feverish to me, but she insisted she wouldn't have anyone stay at home in order to bear her company. For my own part I wouldn't mind staying home. We are bound to run into the Ashtons and if Philip has changed his mind and decides to attend it may be embarrassing.'

'Esther will be fine,' Fanny said. 'She tells me that Patrick and Catherine have already left.'

'And I'd have liked to have ridden with them instead of being cooped up in a silly carriage,' Fausty said, opening the front door and scowling at the vehicle.

'If my cousin wishes to attract a suitor she should behave like a lady and not go galloping all over the countryside.'

'Faith, what a little prude you are, Fanny,' her mother said, laughing. 'Where's the difference between driving yourself to market and riding to the Horse Show? Why, Gobnait's never out of the saddle!'

'And I've not noticed suitors milling around to propose to Gobnait either,' Fanny said. 'Oh, let's not argue, Mother. See the sun is shining and the grass looks as if it's sprinkled with gold dust. It's going to be a marvellous day.'

'And you look lovely,' Fausty said. 'I wager if Henry is there he'll be trying to persuade you to change your mind and wed him after all.'

'Let's not talk any more of suitors, mine or anyone else's,' Fanny smiled. 'Do you think that Gobnait will win the red rosette?'

'No reason why she cannot win all the rosettes,' Fausty said, effectively diverted as Fanny had hoped she would be. 'There isn't a finer horsewoman in the country than Gobnait!'

They were settled by now in the carriage and Fausty rolled down the window to admit the fresh air that blew with an unusual gentleness across the moor.

'We'll be there by mid-morning,' Fanny said.

'Patrick said that he'd a box ordered and he'd arranged for a meal to be served if the rain held off. Otherwise we shall have to go to the tavern with everybody else,' Fausty said. She didn't sound particularly dismayed at the possibility and Fanny sent her a worried glance. For all the sobriety of dark cloak and modest bonnet Fausty looked as if she were out to enjoy herself.

'I sent word the mill hands were to take a couple of hours off,' she was saying. 'I know it's not a public holiday, but don't scold me. The poor dears need a rest.'

'I think it's an excellent idea,' Fanny said warmly. She wished that she had thought of it herself.

'And nobody can deny that the profits are up,' Fausty was continuing. 'Most of that is due to your efforts, my love. It's odd that out of my four children you should be the one with the business sense.'

'Because I'm a female? I don't see why women shouldn't be as proficient as men.'

'No doubt you're right.' Fausty held up her hand as hoofbeats sounded more loudly than the trotting of the carriage horses. A moment later she had her head out of the window and was addressing the rider who had caught up with them.

'Good-morning to you, Mr Wilton. You too are bound for York I take it.'

' 'Morning, ma'am.' The overseer pulled off his hat. 'Yes, we're all making for the Show. They reckon Miss Gobnait will be pulling in all the prizes.'

Fanny had stiffened slightly at the easy familiarity of his tone but her mother, who seemed neither to notice nor resent it, answered cheerfully.

'We expect her to bring home the red rosette. Patrick has decided not to enter this year so Gobnait has a clear field.'

'While Mr Pat concentrates on the drinking! Not to worry, ma'am. I'll likely split a noggin with him myself later on, so I'll see he gets home safe and sound.'

He touched his hand to the brim of his hat in a gesture that might have been insolent and rode on.

'I hope he left someone reliable in charge at

145

the mill,' Fanny said testily.

'Jed Atkins is taking over for the day,' Fausty said. 'There is really no need for you to fret.'

'And he spoke about Patrick as if the two of them were equals. Mother, he may be a good overseer, but I find him a most unpleasant individual.'

'Let's not talk about him now,' Fausty said comfortably, settling herself back against the leather cushions of the seat. 'It is so long since we drove to York. I am determined to let nothing spoil it. Do you think the Grants will join us for lunch?'

'I am hoping that Edward will offer for Gobnait before the day is done,' Fanny said.

'Not if he loses to her in the main event,' Fausty said and laughed at her own witticism.

'Edward is not so small-minded,' Fanny said. 'He would be very proud of her.'

'For my own part,' Fausty murmured, popping a sweetmeat into her mouth, 'I have never noticed anything more than friendship between them, but you may be right. You generally are.'

There was a suspicion of a sigh in her voice, but Fanny didn't hear it.

CHAPTER NINE

The towers of the Minster were silhouetted against the cloudless sky like an omen as they rattled along the track. Fanny, gazing at them through the window of the carriage, decided that they were telling her to concentrate on what she most desired and to ignore petty anxieties. And what she wanted more than anything in the world was to be Philip Ashton's wife. Even the possibility that he might not attend the Show couldn't entirely quench her spirits.

The boxes hired by the gentry were massed on the perimeter of the meadows where the events were to take place. They were little more than seats and tables fixed to wooden railings but the canopies stretched over them afforded shelter from the vagaries of the weather, and the breeze blowing from the river gave a pleasant coolness.

Fausty, alighted from the coach, was in no hurry to isolate herself in the box. Crowds and bustle delighted her and she strolled about on the turf, her quick bright glance darting from one group to the next. There were squires and their ladies, some looking for their boxes while others were greeting friends. Ostlers and stableboys dodged around the horses and traps drawn up at one end of the competition ring

147

while nearer to the river the gypsy caravans were pitched, their occupants splashing bright colour and sham gold against the turf. Fausty looked towards these with a particular pleasure. They reminded her of her girlhood in Ireland when tinkers and didicoys, gay in their impudence and brilliant costumes, came with their trinkets, their jests, and tricks to amuse and cheat the villagers.

Fanny avoided looking in that direction. The gypsies appealed to something in her nature that she kept firmly suppressed. Instead, walking sedately at her mother's side, she bowed and smiled whenever she caught sight of an acquaintance. There was no sign of the Ashtons though servants were carrying a large picnic hamper into their box, but she spotted Gobnait and the uncles leading the mare out onto the turf.

'I must let them know that we've arrived.' Fausty who had spotted them too, headed for them, leaving Fanny to follow or not as she chose.

'There you are! I wondered if you would arrive in time for the preliminary events!'

Elizabeth Grant, in her usual mood of breathless giggles, flitted up. She was wearing a ruffled pink dress that would have been more suitable at an evening occasion, but her face was so distractingly pretty that Fanny wished Patrick would appear. There was no sign of him, however, as Elizabeth linked her hand through the other's arm and swung her about.

'Come and tell me all the gossip. I've seen nothing of you for weeks. Is Esther here?'

'She's at home with a bad cold.'

'Well, she must be feeling pretty dreadful to miss a day out,' Elizabeth said with sympathy. 'Does your cousin have a cold too?'

'No, Catherine is here somewhere.'

'With Patrick, I suppose. Edward was saying that he has scarcely laid eyes on your guest. Patrick keeps her so much to himself.'

'Patrick has to behave as a good host should,' Fanny said. 'You really mustn't mind.'

'Why on earth should I mind?' Elizabeth asked merrily and rattled on, without giving Fanny any chance to reply. 'There is someone else who is not coming today, did you know? They are saying that Philip Ashton quarrelled with his parents and flung out of the house declaring he would never return.'

'They are saying? Who are they?'

'Our parlourmaid had it from her cousin who is a groom at Ashton House. He didn't have the whole of the story because he'd heard it from the under-footman who was crossing the hall and only caught the end of it, but Philip was shouting that he'd not submit to being treated like a child and Lady Ashton had no right to forbid him, and then Philip stalked out and nearly knocked the footman over.'

'Servants' gossip!' Fanny said coldly. 'It was

149

no more than a storm in a teacup, I'll wager.'

'Well, Philip isn't here,' Elizabeth said with an air of triumph. 'Henry is, though. Do tell me if it's true, Fanny. Do you and Henry Ashton have an understanding?'

'Is that what "they" are saying?' Fanny enquired. 'If so you may give them the lie. Henry Ashton and I are good friends, but there is nothing more than that between us. I have no wish to become a clergyman's wife.'

'I wonder if Henry can be persuaded to tell us what the quarrel was about,' Elizabeth said.

'It would be gross bad manners to ask,' Fanny said quickly. 'Surely you don't wish to acquire the reputation of being a gossip who heeds servants' tales?'

'No, of course not.' Elizabeth, who fortunately was easily diverted, squeezed her friend's arm and said, 'Are you going to wager on Gobnait or Edward to win the red rosette? I know I ought to wager on my brother but I think that Gobnait will take the palm, don't you?'

'She probably will,' Fanny agreed. There was a faint gloom in her tone. Gobnait might be a splendid horsewoman but until she learned to be more feminine it was unlikely she would receive any offers of marriage.

The preliminary events, most of them featuring small children mounted on their ponies, were already under way in the smaller of the two rings marked out for the programme. The main events were to take place after luncheon and only those who had children competing took an interest in these early jump-offs and trotting races.

'Shall we go and have our fortunes told?' Elizabeth asked. 'I had mine told last year.'

'None of it is true,' Fanny began, but her friend interrupted.

'Oh, but it is! Well, some of it is, anyway. You remember Cecilia Dare, who married that Scottish gentleman and went to live over the border?'

'He was not a gentleman. He was a wine merchant.'

'Was he truly? From his manner one could not have guessed it,' Elizabeth said with interest. 'The point is that Cecilia was told by a fortune teller that she would marry a dark-haired foreigner.'

'He came from Glasgow,' Fanny objected.

'Well, that's near,' Elizabeth said, 'and he was most certainly dark-haired, so there is something to it, you see?'

Fanny, making some non-committal noise, found herself wondering if she could endure Elizabeth as a sister-in-law. Pretty and vivacious her friend might be but there was no denying that she was fearfully silly. Fortunately gentlemen seldom seemed to trouble about such things.

As if thought had summoned him Patrick strolled towards them. To Fanny's displeasure

151

Catherine was clinging to his arm. The Irish girl wore the bonnet and cloak that Fanny had given her but fine clothes could not turn her into a lady. Already her shoes were scuffed and her hair was coming out of curl. Patrick, however, seemed not to notice. He was chatting to his companion with more animation than he usually displayed and greeted the two young ladies casually.

'We wondered why you were late,' Fanny said. 'Elizabeth was beginning to feel quite shamefully neglected.'

'My horse cast a shoe and we had to ride double,' Catherine said. 'It was such a lovely morning, Fanny, and then I got the devil's own thirst on me so Patrick made me stop off at a little tavern on the edge of the town and we drank some port wine.'

'In the morning! Patrick, you ought to have known better,' Fanny said crossly. 'You will have Cousin Catherine quite tipsy.'

'Why, bless you but a drop of port never hurt anyone,' Catherine said, looking amused. 'At home wasn't I practically weaned on the uncles' poteen!'

No, she was not a lady. Patrick, however, seemed not one whit embarrassed on her account and Elizabeth, leaving Fanny's side, held out her hand to Catherine saying laughingly, 'My name is Elizabeth Grant and I am neighbour to your cousins. Tell me what this poteen is. Do you think that your uncles would make some for me?'

'Come and ask them,' Patrick invited.

He had linked arms with Elizabeth now but Catherine, at his other side, made no attempt to disengage herself. 'Tell Mother that I'll see her later,' Patrick said over his shoulder as they walked away.

For a moment Fanny felt a surge of indignation at having been thus abandoned. Then she shook off the mood, reminding herself that at least Patrick and Elizabeth were together and no doubt they would find some tactful way of shaking off Catherine without hurting her feelings. Meanwhile the morning was bright and there was plenty to see. She unfurled her cream umbrella and, thus shaded from the heat, walked slowly across the turf.

The Ashtons were in their box. It was impossible to miss Lady Ashton's purple bonnet in which two ostrich feathers strove for mastery. At her side Sir John and Henry looked crushed despite their top hats. Philip wasn't there. The pretty little scene she had rehearsed in her mind melted like snow in April. She had not known how greatly she had counted on his being there to appreciate the look of silent sympathy she bestowed, the tact with which she turned the conversation to happier themes. Then she cheered herself by remembering that it was scarcely noon. Perhaps he would arrive in time for the main events.

Meanwhile, catching Lady Ashton's basilisk gaze fixed upon her, she paused briefly to bow and smile before continuing her stroll.

Fausty, having duly admired the horse, wished her daughter luck and cautioned her brothers against partaking too liberally of the liquid refreshments, and walked on briskly, greeting acquaintances. It was a little sad when she cared to reflect on it to realize that she had no truly intimate friends. Such was the insularity of the county that after twenty years she was still spoken of as the Irish girl whom Earl Sabre had brought home as his bride. And as Sabre Hall stood somewhat isolated there were not many opportunities for social occasions, and as Fausty had been a widow with four children to rear she was only included when an extra female was required to make up the numbers. Fortunately her nature was not particularly reflective and she had the great gift of extracting pleasure from small events.

Life, she thought now, had become more interesting. It was good to have her brothers visiting though she had to admit that they were shiftless, but being younger than herself she was still apt to think of them as the tousle-headed boys she had left in Ireland when she had travelled to England to make her way in the world. It was good to see them again and to have news of her family and Catherine was a darling girl. It was odd that of the eight

Sullivans who had grown up together in the cabin on the outskirts of Dublin only herself should have prospered. The mill, thanks to careful management, brought in an increasing profit. If, as she hoped, Patrick began to take a serious interest in his cousin then he might settle down and make a success of the business. It was not right that Fanny should be beset by responsibility. The thought of Fanny clouded the day a little. Dear, pretty Fanny was so earnest and hard-working, the ant to Esther's moth. Fausty wished she could feel happier about the two betrothals so secretly made and so abruptly broken, but she had the uneasy feeling that more lay behind the events than she had been told. Philip had seemed so sincere when he had told her of his love for Esther and Henry would have made such a good husband for Fanny. It was a great pity that nothing had come of it.

'Tell your fortune, lady.' A ragged woman with a sulky mouth and a crimson bodice had stepped out from the shadow of a small tent and was gazing at her brightly.

Fausty glanced about but Fanny was nowhere to be seen. 'If you please,' she said.

'If *you* please, lady,' the other promptly returned. 'It's my trade to please you by unrolling the future.'

'And if the future's a bad one am I still expected to be pleased?' Fausty enquired, following as the woman re-entered the tent.

'You've a lucky face, lady. Your future will be a bright one.'

'And even brighter if I cross your palm with silver?' Fausty did so and seated herself at one of the stools with which the interior was littered, holding out her hand.

'Both, pretty lady. The left for the destiny born within you and the right for the way you've dealt with it.'

The gypsy had also seated herself and was studying Fausty's palms in the light that slanted through the open tent flap.

'You lost your husband,' she pronounced.

'Not hard to guess since I'm in mourning,' Fausty said, amused.

'Which you've worn longer than custom says,' the gypsy continued. 'And I could have found that out by asking around too, but I didn't! You've grown children and a handsome home and you're still young enough to find another lover.'

'All of which I could have told you myself. What of the future?'

'There'll be joy and sorrow in equal measure and the three children born to bring both. One not to be known and the other two not bearing the name but in the family all the same. I see a voyage across the sea and a dark man with tinker blood. I see—'

'Not much,' Fausty said, disappointed.

'Three children,' the fortune teller repeated. 'I see them plain. Others too, but

156

they are not so plain. And the lover to bring you happiness. But treachery too. There is treachery in the smile of a daughter.'

'And that's enough for one afternoon,' Fausty interrupted, rising and pulling her hands away. It was foolish but some hypnotic quality in the other's voice disturbed her.

'Take care, pretty lady.' The gypsy made no attempt to stop her leaving and there was the flush of a frown across the dark face as the woman leaned back.

It had been a silly impulse that led her to agree to having her palm read! The woman had been a charlatan like so many of her kind and what she had said was sheer nonsense. Tinker lovers and voyages across the sea and treachery in the smile of a daughter? That last was most certainly untrue and the other happenings were less than likely.

Fausty, catching her foot in a tussock of grass, stumbled, swore, and was prevented from falling by the grasp of a tall man who held her upright as she strove to regain her balance.

'You've maybe taken a drop too much on an empty stomach, ma'am,' a voice said laughingly.

'I've not taken a drop of anything at all!' Fausty exclaimed indignantly, freeing herself and almost stumbling again.

'Then you'll be needing something now,' the stranger said. 'Will you do me the favour of taking a glass of wine with me?'

'With a stranger?' Fausty tried desperately to retain some semblance of dignity but the man who smiled down at her was young and handsome with a decided twinkle in his black eyes and her protest ended in a giggle.

'Allow me to introduce myself, ma'am.' He stepped away a pace and swept off his hat to reveal close-cropped dark curls. 'My name is Matthew Lawley and I am entirely at your service.'

'Faustina Sabre.' She gave him her hand, amusement still sparkling in her eyes.

'And you just had your fortune told.'

'On a foolish impulse.' She felt herself blushing. 'The woman talked a lot of nonsense.'

'They generally do.' He had retained his clasp of her fingers. 'Now I can tell better fortunes, for there's a tradition in my family that a travelling tinker got over the wall when my grandfather was away.'

'A tinker!' She looked at him with sharp suspicion but he was taking her arm and leading her away from the tent towards the refreshment booth without a backward glance.

'We've been respectable ever since,' he assured her.

'Do you live in York?' she enquired.

'I'm visiting.' He flashed her another sideways look. 'I regret that I am one of those reprehensible persons known as gentlemen of leisure. I'm staying with friends in Doncaster for a few days, but they had a prior engagement to fulfil so I came over for the day to have a little wager and then to find myself a pretty companion with whom to share my winnings.'

'Then you should find a pretty *young* companion,' she felt bound to say.

'Age is how you feel and how you feel shows in your face,' he asserted. 'Which makes you about twenty-three years old. How old are you?'

'Twenty-three,' she answered promptly and laughed, flinging back her head and letting the merriment ripple out of her.

'You ought to wear a green bonnet,' he said suddenly. 'An emerald green bonnet to match your accent and bring out the glints in your eyes.'

'And that tinker you mentioned must have had Irish blood and a free ticket to the Blarney Stone!' she retorted.

'Any man would tell you that you shouldn't wear mourning unless you have a mourning heart and it's clear that you haven't,' he said, smiling at her as if he dared contradiction.

She was in no mood to contradict. There had swept over her the joy and recklessness of her girlhood and she felt as if, given the chance, she would have flung off her black dress and capered in her petticoat. It was clear that Matthew Lawley had not realized that she was a member of the gentry but had taken her to be a tradesman's widow with whom a gentleman might behave with rather more freedom than with a lady. The mistake which would have mortified Fanny caused Fausty the liveliest amusement.

'If you'll take a seat I'll bring the refreshments,' Matthew Lawley was saying.

Fausty, smiling an assent, looked involuntarily past his tall figure and met Fanny's astonished blue gaze. Her daughter, straight as a ramrod in her sable-trimmed cloak, had paused beneath the striped awning.

'I am so very sorry,' Fausty heard herself stammer, 'and you must think me very rude, but it is quite impossible for me to accept. I have to leave at once.'

'But you said—,' he began.

'A mistake,' she said. 'Forgive me but I am needed elsewhere.'

She thrust past him with a rudeness of which normally she would have been incapable and hurried out into the open where, within a few seconds, she was swallowed up in the crowd. At her side Fanny said, an accusation in her voice, 'Who was that young gentleman? He is not local, is he?'

'A visitor, staying at Doncaster,' Fausty said, walking more rapidly. She dared not turn her head to see if he had followed her.

'What were you doing in the refreshment tent?' Fanny persisted.

160

Fausty had a momentary impulse to reply smartly, 'Waiting to have a glass of wine with a view to seduction later on.'

'It was shady there,' she answered and entered her own box with relief. With her black umbrella fixed to the rung of her chair to provide shade she was sufficiently concealed from the gaze of any passer-by to be able to look about herself, but there was no sign of Matthew Lawley. Presumably he had gone in search of more willing game. Heaving a small sigh she decided it was as well. After twenty years without a man she would last out a little longer without having to take the first man who displayed an interest in her.

'Gobnait is snatching a bite while she exercises the mare,' Patrick informed them, coming up with Catherine on his arm.

Fanny, irritated to see no Elizabeth and still puzzled by the brief glimpse she had had of her mother's flushed and smiling face as she talked to the stranger, said sharply, 'Gobnait has plenty of time to eat a civilized luncheon before she exercises the horse! Soon she will be demanding a bag of oats just like the mare.'

'Oh, Fanny, you're so comical,' Catherine exclaimed, coming to sit next to her.

'Are Sean and Stevie coming?' Fausty enquired.

'They went to the tavern,' Patrick said, swinging a leg over the low rail.

'Well, if they don't hurry we shall eat

161

everything,' she said placidly, beginning to lift the food out of the basket.

Huldah had provided an excellent assortment of pies and cakes, with a covered bowl filled with salad and bread rolls wrapped in a large napkin. There was lemonade too and four bottles of claret, but her twin brothers had evidently decided that it would be more amusing to sample the hospitality of the tavern. Patrick, on the other hand, seemed content to remain with the family. Watching him as he sprawled on the grass next to Catherine's chair, Fausty found herself hoping again that the influence of her niece could cause him to settle down more contentedly than he had in the past. It was time that he took an interest in Sabre Mill. With Patrick at the helm she and Fanny would have more leisure.

I might travel, Fausty thought, biting with relish into a chicken leg. Glory be, after twenty years of rearing my family and being buried alive at Sabre Mill, haven't I the right to enjoy myself a little?

She had not spoken aloud so nobody answered, but her glance towards Fanny was tinged with guilt all the same.

Her brothers returned for the main events and one look at their unsteady gait and flushed faces made her thankful that they were not competing. Gobnait, having taken her lunch with only the mare for company, now reappeared mounted, the scarlet of her hair

162

competing—some would have said clashing— with the darker red of her riding-habit. The other young ladies who were taking part were more sedately clad in habits of blue serge and black broadcloth, their hair wound neatly under little tricorn hats decorated with white plumes. Gobnait's curly mane hung down her back and in defiance of fashion she wore a scarf tied over her head. Yet many of the glances that followed her slim, upright figure were admiring and the fact that Gobnait herself was supremely indifferent to such glances only served to increase her attraction.

The others had left the box and were crowding to the tiered benches round the larger enclosure. Fanny hung back. It was not, she told herself, that she was jealous of her sister. Fanny had no desire to compete in the show-ring or to draw men's eyes in the way that Gobnait did. There was a crude vitality about the tall, flame-haired girl mounted on the shining mare that reminded her of the gypsy caravans with their gay, ragged occupants. Both disturbed her for reasons she didn't fully understand.

The Ashton box was deserted. Henry had evidently been more offended at her refusal than she had realized, and decided to ignore her, but it was not Henry she had wanted to see. Philip would not be coming and the opportunity of speaking to him was delayed. She became aware that someone in the crowd had paused and was looking at her intently. For an instant she felt a little thrill of pleasure. Then, as she recognized the strange young gentleman with whom her mother had been laughing, her spine stiffened and she turned away with an air of what she liked to think of as dignified coolness.

'Miss Gobnait's starting her round!' Joe Wilton, his hat pushed to the back of his head, was addressing her in a loud voice that made her flush scarlet with temper. He had obviously been drinking otherwise he would have shown more respect, she decided, and nodded to him briefly as she began to walk rapidly towards the enclosure.

He caught up with her in a couple of strides, laying his hand on her arm.

'All by herself, is she?' His voice was slightly blurred and his breath stank of rum. 'Little Miss Fanny all by herself and deserted by her family.'

'Wilton, you've drunk too much,' she said, shaking her arm free and walking more rapidly.

'Isn't the overseer entitled to a day's pleasure?' he enquired. A faint whine had crept into his voice, but at the back of his small eyes something red glowed briefly and was gone.

'Not if you become insolent and objectionable,' she said icily. 'Go and drink some black coffee, Wilton, and sober up.'

'Is that what you say to your brother?' he mocked. 'Is that what you tell him to do when he comes staggering home after a night's carouse?'

'That's enough!' She gave him a furious glance and, seeing with relief that they were on the fringe of the crowd, quickened her pace further. Wilton, however, was still at her heels and his hand had shot out again to fasten on her waist. The surface amiability of his mood had passed and his vicious temper, of which she had heard but never witnessed, was rising. Pressed close against him by the crowd she could smell not only the rum he had drunk but the sweat that was beginning to run down his heavy face.

'That's not polite, Miss Fanny,' Wilton said, lowering his voice. 'This is a holiday and you ought to be polite to your neighbours!'

'You are an employee, not a neighbour,' she said tensely, 'and were it not for the fact that I am convinced the drink has affected your brain, you would be dismissed this moment.'

'Ah, you'll not dismiss me, Miss Fanny.' He laid a finger alongside his nose and leered at her. 'You need me to keep the mill going so that the profits keep rolling in and you can buy pretty gowns and run after the younger gentlemen.'

Cold rage at his daring to speak thus to her made her speechless for a moment. The spectators were applauding and a bystander called out, 'A faultless round, by God! That young lady rides better than any man I ever saw!'

'You're dismissed.' Her voice was as cutting as her glance. 'You may go to Mr Leigh and collect one month's pay, but don't come to the mill apart from that.'

'It's not your mill and you can't give me notice,' he returned.

'My brother will dismiss you.' She turned and pushed her way to the rail, hearing his scornful laughter as he swayed behind her.

'Gobnait will win!' Catherine was jumping up and down with excitement. 'Truly there is nobody who can come near her now! Isn't she a splendid girl! Poor Esther will be so sorry to have missed this.'

'Patrick, I want you to dismiss Joe Wilton.' Fanny spoke directly to her brother. 'He is disgustingly intoxicated and he has grossly insulted me. I want you to dismiss him immediately, do you hear?'

'If he's taken a drop too much he'll have forgotten it by morning,' Patrick began.

'I will not have forgotten and neither will any of the people who heard him!' Fanny blazed. 'Promise me that you will dismiss him! Promise me!'

'I promise, I promise.' He gave her a long-suffering look for spoiling the tranquillity of the day and turned his attention to the horses again.

CHAPTER TEN

'Didn't you say that Gobnait would win the red rosette?' Fausty demanded of Fanny and Catherine as they drove home.

Gobnait herself had elected to return in the horse-box with the uncles, an arrangement that Fanny had viewed with some trepidation, both of them half-foxed. Patrick, who had remained sober, however, was accompanying them and, as Fausty seemed unconcerned, she held her tongue.

'She rides like an angel,' Catherine said.

'Ah! That's the Irish blood in her,' Fausty said.

'Surely Father was an excellent horseman?' Fanny interposed.

'That he was,' Fausty agreed, 'even though he didn't have a drop of Irish blood in him. Fanny, what's this Patrick was telling me about you wanting to dismiss Joe Wilton?'

'He was disgustingly intoxicated and he insulted me,' Fanny said, her face flushing with remembered temper. 'This is not the first time either. He has always been rude and mocking, and there comes a limit! You recall him, Catherine, when we went to the mill? He was exceedingly disrespectful then.'

'He frightened me,' Catherine admitted.

'I cannot think how we can replace him,'

Fausty said. 'He's been our overseer for more than ten years.'

'Mother, there are equally good men who could take on the same duties and be far more pleasant about it,' Fanny said impatiently. 'You cannot like to have me set at nought by a ruffian like Joe Wilton!'

'Of course not, dear.' Fausty spoke mildly, having no wish for an argument.

The day had been a pleasant one. The Ashtons had bowed with a polite reserve that had left Fausty feeling relieved that she was not a guest after all in their box and her other neighbours had all expressed great pleasure at seeing her. Gobnait had carried off the prize and Patrick had hardly left his cousin's side all day. Her full lips curved into a smile as she thought of the dark-haired stranger who had made her feel like a young girl again. It was as well that Fanny had interrupted else she might have been tempted to behave recklessly. She leaned back, closing her eyes and pushing away the uneasy reflection that Joe Wilton might not take too kindly to the idea of losing his position. Patrick would have to handle it, and the necessity of having to do so might prove the spur that drove him to take a proper interest in the running of the mill. Taken all round, she decided sleepily, the Horse Show had been a great success.

Fanny was tired too and more disappointed in the day's events than she would admit. She had hoped so much to see Philip, but there had been no sign of him and the pleasure she might have had had been further eroded by the nasty little incident with Wilton and by Patrick's close squiring of Catherine. She was glad when the lamps of Sabre Hall gleamed through the dark and they swung around to the back of the house where Huldah held open the kitchen door, calling as they alighted.

'Did Gobnait win? I'll be bound she beat everybody into a cocked hat!'

'That she did,' Fausty assured her.

'The red rosette!' Huldah clapped her plump hands. 'Didn't I always say there was nobody to touch her?'

'Except Patrick,' Catherine put in shyly.

'Patrick wasn't competing,' Fanny said a trifle crossly, 'so the question doesn't arise.'

'The food you gave us was marvellous,' Fausty said quickly. 'There's none of it left.'

'I didn't pack it so you could lug it all home again,' Huldah said, looking pleased. 'I daresay you'll be wanting supper when everyone's home?'

'I'll help,' Catherine offered.

'That's very kind of you, Miss,' Huldah beamed.

'I'll go and see how Esther's feeling,' Fanny began.

'I took her some supper a little while since,' Huldah said. 'She's been asleep most of the day. I looked in at her around noon but she'd gone back to bed and said she didn't need anything.'

'She's not worse?' Fanny asked in alarm.

'She ate all her supper,' Huldah reassured her.

'I'll run up and see her.' Fanny went swiftly through to the hall and up the main staircase.

She had forgotten Esther during the hours at the Show and her conscience smote her a little as she hastened up to the gallery. Esther was not fond of crowds and excitement but it must have been very dull for her all alone all day.

At the door she tapped, waited a moment and then went in, seeing by the light of the lamp that Esther had left burning that the room was in its usual cluttered state. Her twin was not in bed but seated in a low chair by the unshuttered window, her attitude one of unconscious yearning.

'Esther, Huldah said you were asleep,' Fanny went in, closing the door.

'I woke up again,' Esther said, not turning her head.

With her chin on her hand and her hair feathering her temples Esther's profile had a gentle, dreaming quality.

'Are you feeling better?' Fanny asked.

'I'm feeling fine.' Esther glanced at her and smiled. There was a fleeting wildness in the smile that frightened the other for a moment but the look was gone as Esther added calmly,

170

'You mustn't fret about me, Fanny. I'm feeling very much better, truly.'

'Gobnait won the red rosette,' Fanny said.

'I knew she would,' Esther said in the same calm, even tone. 'She's the best horsewoman in the county.'

'The Ashtons.' Fanny hesitated, then went on brightly. 'I begin to think we have both had a fortunate escape. Henry is so cold and stiff, and Lady Ashton—well, if she were not who she is I'd be tempted to describe her as vulgar. Honestly, if you had seen her purple—'

'Please, do you mind if we don't discuss the Ashtons?' Esther put in.

'Then we won't.' Fanny patted her sister's arm. 'Edward Grant was runner-up to Gobnait but he didn't seem to mind very much. If only she could be persuaded to take him he would prove a most amiable husband.'

'I don't believe that Gobnait has met the man she wishes to marry yet,' Esther said.

'Edward and she would suit perfectly,' Fanny argued. 'Really, Esther, you go about in such a dream that your opinion can scarcely be regarded as infallible.'

'I never thought it was,' Esther said calmly and gave a sudden trill of laughter that caused the other to glance at her in the fear that she might, after all, have a fever.

'Perhaps you ought to go back to bed,' Fanny said. 'These summer colds can turn nasty quite suddenly. Get a good night's sleep

171

and I'll see you in the morning.'

'You worry about me too much,' Esther said, placidly rising.

'You're my twin,' Fanny said warmly, 'and I was blessed with a worrying nature!'

She blew Esther a kiss and went out again. Something in her sister's manner troubled her but she couldn't define exactly what it was.

The gallery was shadowed, the bright rectangles of sunshine turned now to moonlight. Two figures stood in a patch of darkness, arms entwined in what was clearly a swift and passionate embrace. They broke apart as Fanny closed the bedroom door and Catherine hurried off with her head bent.

Fanny, who had hesitated in embarrassment, walked towards her brother, her fists clenching with indignation.

'Patrick, you promised that you'd not drink too much,' she began.

'I'm as sober as a judge—more sober than most of the judges I know,' he said easily, not one whit abashed.

'Then you should behave like a gentleman,' she said. 'Cousin Catherine is a guest and should be treated as one.'

'And you, my dear sister, are a prude!' he retorted. 'You're also a busybody. It's none of your business what I do or whom I choose to kiss!'

'Uncle Stephen and Uncle Sean would likely be angry if they knew you were insulting poor Catherine.'

'Uncle Sean and Uncle Stevie don't give a toss how I spend my time,' Patrick grinned, 'and since when has kissing been an insult? If you want my opinion, Fanny, it's time somebody came along and insulted you so thoroughly that you'd not time to worry about other people's affairs!'

'I don't want your opinion,' Fanny said coldly. 'All I know is that your flirting with Catherine would hurt poor Elizabeth dreadfully if it came to her ears.'

'What on earth has my kissing Catherine got to do with Elizabeth?' he demanded.

'Only that everyone knows that sooner or later you and Elizabeth will marry.'

'The only one who "knows" that is yourself,' Patrick said impatiently. 'Elizabeth has as little interest in me as I have in her. Why don't you stop trying to marry people off, Fanny? That's occupation for a dried-up spinster, not a pretty girl.'

Fanny shrugged away the hand he laid on her arm and went crossly down the stairs. She was not sure why she felt so irritable save that the people she loved seemed to be slipping away from her and events had begun to run along paths she couldn't follow.

Morning brought no relief from the problems that nagged at her. She had slept too heavily and the inside of her head felt as if it had been stuffed with cotton wool. She dressed

173

and came downstairs with less than her usual briskness, to meet Huldah on her way to the kitchen.

'Everybody's still abed,' the latter said with a sniff that indicated her opinion of folk who lay in bed after a day's pleasure. 'I can make you some breakfast in a moment.'

'I only want a cup of coffee. Are they all still asleep?'

'I took your mother a cup of tea, but I've no doubt she turned over and went straight back to sleep,' Huldah informed her. 'I think Patrick must have gone out for an early gallop. The back door was unlocked when I came down.'

'I think I'll drive to the mill,' Fanny said, going past her into the kitchen.

'To find out if Joe Wilton has collected his wages?' Huldah enquired. 'Your mother told me about it last night.'

'And you're disapproving, I suppose?' Fanny poured coffee for herself and sat down at one end of the well-scrubbed table.

'Wilton's a nasty piece of work,' Huldah said calmly. 'I still think it would be more fitting if you keep away from that mill. I never did believe that females should go into business like men.'

'Someone has to take an interest. Anyway Mother has been running it for years!'

'Your mother was forced to it when your father died,' Huldah said. 'Now it's for Patrick to take over.'

'Patrick is going to dismiss Wilton this morning. That's probably where he went so early.'

'Then why not leave it to him?'

'Because I feel like some air.' Fanny swallowed the last of her coffee and stood up. 'I've also got a headache and I don't intend living my life according to your instructions.'

'Hoity-toity!' Huldah made a small face at her and went through to the pantry.

Fanny harnessed Belle and backed the pony between the shafts of the trap. The other horses regarded her solemnly from their stalls. As far as Fanny could tell none were missing which meant that Patrick must have returned from his ride. The possibility that he hadn't yet kept his promise crossed her mind, but she shook it off as she climbed up into the driving-seat. It would do no harm to make certain if she chanced to drive in that vicinity. Also in her mind was the possibility that Philip might have decided to take a morning gallop. It was not possible that he would stay away from the district for much longer.

The morning was bright, the rain still holding off. She drove briskly, her headache fading as the breeze lifted the curls from her temples and cooled her face. Below, the mill gave the impression of having spread itself out for inspection and the cottages straggling up the hill were toy houses.

The millyard was deserted but, as she drove

through the gateway, the overseer emerged from the weaving-shed and called an impudent, 'Morning, Miss.'

'What are you doing here?' She drew up and frowned at him.

'Doing my work. Where else should a man be but at his work?' he enquired, hooking his thumbs in his belt and squinting at her.

'You were dismissed,' she reminded him. 'I told you to collect your money.'

'I didn't figure you meant it,' he began, but she interrupted him angrily.

'Of course I meant it! I'm not in the habit of saying what I don't mean! Go to Mr Leigh and get your money at once and then be off the premises.'

'You've no right to go giving the orders. Mr Patrick is master.'

'I speak for my brother,' she said loftily.

'You'd speak for the whole world, you!' he said angrily. 'You've no call to lose me my place, not after the years I've worked for this family! I started as a little lad and you'll not find a better overseer anywhere in Yorkshire!'

'Nor a ruder, harsher one! I shall employ someone more suited to our expectations.'

'And throw my family out to starve!'

'I'll see that my brother writes you a good reference,' Fanny said reluctantly.

'You can keep your reference,' he said sullenly. 'I'm not leaving because you can't make me, and it's no good you talking to your

176

brother. I've only to stand Mr Patrick a round at the tavern and he'll be eating out of my hand in about five minutes, so you can turn around and go home again, Missy.'

Without thought she grabbed up her riding-crop and struck out at him, her face contorted with temper. An instant more and she was jerked from her seat and found herself struggling with the burly overseer. Belle whickered nervously, shying away and from somewhere Thomas Leigh's high, cracked voice sounded in alarm.

Another figure interposed. She was flung back against the side of the trap as the crop was wrenched from her and the newcomer proceeded to belabour Wilton about the head and shoulders with its butt.

'Patrick, thank God! He attacked me when I told him that his dismissal still stood,' Fanny gasped out thankfully.

'I seen it, Mr Patrick!' Thomas Leigh panted from the counting-house. 'An unprovoked attack on a defenceless young lady! I can testify to that.'

'Defenceless? She's a hellcat!' Joe Wilton, blood streaming from the deep cuts on his face, staggered to his feet, his fists clenched. 'By God, but you'd better tame her quick else none of your lives will be worth the living!'

'Leigh, give him what money's due to him, then see him off the premises,' Patrick ordered.

'I'll send the wife to collect it. As for you, Miss—' Wilton turned on Fanny so threateningly that she shrank back.

'One more word to my sister and you'll not get up again,' Patrick said loudly. His normally pale face was flushed with anger and a lock of his red hair tumbled over his forehead. He brushed it back impatiently, gripping the crop and staring down at the shorter, thicker-set man.

'This isn't the last of it,' Wilton said at last, turning on his heel and shuffling away. The glance he sent over his shoulder was a chilling one.

'Oh, Patrick, I'm so glad you came,' Fanny said tremulously.

'What possessed you to start an argument with him?' asked Patrick, anger still in his face.

'Argument! I wouldn't lower myself to argue,' Fanny said. Her strong desire to burst into tears had fled and her voice was indignant. 'I drove down to make certain he'd accepted his dismissal and he insulted me all over again.'

'Attacked her, as I can testify,' Thomas Leigh put in. 'Will you be pressing charges, Mr Patrick?'

'No need to make a mountain out of a mole hill,' Patrick said. 'See that his wife gets the money due to him. I'll drive my sister home.'

He turned to tie his own mount to the back of the trap while the clerk still hovered, torn between anxiety and excitement.

'Would Miss Fanny prefer to come into my office for a few moments? She looks quite badly shocked.'

'I shall be perfectly all right, Mr Leigh.' Fanny spoke stiffly as she climbed tremblingly up into the high seat. Patrick, having secured the horse, joined her, taking the reins himself and edging her across to the passenger seat. There were still patches of colour on his cheekbones but she sensed he was as annoyed with her as with Joe Wilton, so sat meekly, gripping the side of the trap as they drove out to the track again.

'Put your bonnet straight,' Patrick ordered tersely. 'You look as if you've been in a wrestling match.'

'I might have been seriously hurt,' she said in a small voice.

'You would probably have received the spanking you deserve,' he answered. 'Why cannot you keep your nose out of other people's business, Fanny?'

'The mill is my business, and I thought—'

'You thought I might forget all about dismissing Joe Wilton if you were not around to keep me up to the mark.'

'I'm very sorry, Patrick,' she said contritely.

'Not that I'd much choice after what just happened,' he admitted. 'I shall put Hampton in his stead.'

'Sam Hampton?'

'Unless you've another candidate in mind?'

'Sam will make a fine overseer,' she said.

'And in future leave the mill to me.'

'I'd do so gladly if only you would take a real interest in it,' Fanny said earnestly. 'But you never have.'

'Then in future I'd better, before you have another quarrel with one of my hands—not that I'd much liking for Wilton. The man's a bit of a brute and I won't stand for having my little sister insulted.'

He flashed her a smile that invited conciliation.

'You must persuade Thomas Leigh to retire,' she urged. 'He cannot keep the accounts as efficiently as he used to, and his penmanship is becoming shaky. I've talked to Mother about it. We could offer him a small pension and he has no family.'

'He has only his job at the mill,' Patrick said. There was a note in his voice that puzzled her. He sounded almost as if he pitied her and not the clerk.

'He's very obstinate,' she began.

'Leave it, Fan. One dismissal is sufficient for a morning,' he interrupted.

'But you will take an interest in the business in future? You never have until now.'

'Provided you keep your fingers out of my pie.'

'I was so thankful when you came.' She spoke warmly, pleasure stirring in her at the memory of his anger on her behalf. She had not realized how fond of her Patrick was under his mask of careless indifference. This episode might mark the beginning of a new closeness between them, as well as jolting him out of his apathy.

'You were fortunate,' he said wryly. 'Huldah told me you'd scooted down to the mill when I came down for breakfast.'

'Came down? Hadn't you been down already?' she enquired in surprise.

'I slept like a log all night,' he informed her.

'Someone went out and left the kitchen door open. Huldah was grumbling about it.'

'Probably one of the uncles. The girls and mother are still in bed. Even Gobnait slept over this morning.'

'Patrick.' Taking advantage of the new cordiality between them she spoke placatingly. 'Patrick, I'm sorry I interfered last night. It was none of my business if you wanted to kiss Catherine.'

'Very true,' he agreed.

'Only she might be inclined to read more into it than you intended.'

'As to that.' He glanced at her, then shook his head. 'Never mind, Fanny. We'll call truce and you can tell me all about the business and how to run it.'

She sensed that he was laughing at her but it was a small price to pay for their new harmony, and the rest of the drive passed pleasantly.

Helping her down when they arrived back in the stableyard he said, 'We'll keep this morning's little episode to ourselves. Mother will only fuss if she hears I've been brawling with the overseer.'

'You've made an enemy there and it's partly my fault.'

'Not to worry. Joe Wilton is all muscle and wind,' he said easily, giving her a slight slap on her rump as Huldah opened the kitchen door. Her broad face was flushed, her voice anxious as she called, 'You didn't run across Esther on your way back, did you?'

'Esther? No, why?' Fanny rustled into the kitchen.

'Because she's not in the house,' Huldah said.

'Not in the house? Don't be silly. She must be.'

'She's not. I took breakfast up in the end and she isn't there.'

'Cousin Catherine is sharing her room. She must know where she is,' Fanny said, going through to the hall.

Catherine, hurrying down the stairs with Fausty at her heels, said in agitation, 'But I don't, Fanny. I didn't wake up until quite late and she wasn't there. She isn't upstairs.'

'Then she's gone for a walk. You know how she likes wandering about on the moors,' Fanny began.

'After a heavy cold that's the worst possible thing she could do,' Fausty said crossly. 'Gobnait, is there any sign of her?'

The elder girl, a wrapper thrown about her shoulders and her hair still in its night pigtail, called from the gallery.

'Not a trace. I went through to the loft. The uncles are up, but they've not seen her.'

'She must have gone out early then. You said that you found the kitchen door open, Huldah?'

'She didn't go in the direction of the mill,' Patrick said, joining them. 'I'd have seen her.'

'Perhaps she strolled in the other direction towards Batley Tor,' Gobnait suggested. 'I'll get dressed and ride that way.'

'She ought not to have gone out at all,' Fausty said. 'Did you see her last evening? Fanny, you did! You said she was feeling better.'

'She seemed better,' Fanny said slowly. In her mind there was rising the image of her sister's profile and the swift wild look she had cast. To stem a tiny quiver of apprehension she said. 'Has she taken anything with her?'

'I never thought to look,' Catherine said helplessly.

Fanny uttered an impatient exclamation and pushed past her, running up the staircase and along the gallery to where the door of Esther's room stood ajar. The room was wildly untidy, mainly littered with Esther's things, with

Catherine's few possessions squeezed among them. A glance at both the unmade beds told her nothing and it was impossible to tell at one look if any of Esther's clothes were missing from the cluttered dresser or the wardrobe crammed with dresses. There were various cloaks and scarves strewn over the backs of chairs and the stool by the window and the fireplace was choked with reddish grey cinders. Fanny gazed round, wondering how on earth her twin could endure to live in the midst of such disorder. There was nothing to indicate what garments Esther had worn and no sign of the nightdress in which she had been clad the previous day. Her purse, coins spilling out of it, lay on the table amid a welter of feather fans, lengths of lace and silk ribbon, and posies of artificial flowers. A slip of paper caught her attention and she picked it up and unfolded it curiously. Esther's round, childish handwriting leapt up at her, each word a hammer blow between the eyes.

'Dearest Fanny,
'Tell them all how sorry I am, but this is all I can do. There's nothing else. E.'

'What is it?' Fausty, hurrying in after her, snatched the paper and read it, her eyes dilating with shock as she took in the meaning.
'She's killed herself. Holy Mother of God, she's gone off and killed herself.'

184

'We don't know that,' Fanny said, trying to speak calmly. 'We don't know where she is.'

'She'll have drowned herself down in the river!' Fausty cried. 'Or hanged herself in the barn!'

There was no mistaking the sincerity of her alarm but her highly-coloured dramatic way of expressing herself struck a discordant note.

Fanny said sharply, crushing down her alarm, 'That's foolishness, Mother. Esther's writing this note means nothing. If she went out then I'll wager she'll be back before noon!'

'But she says—why would she do such a terrible thing?'

'Esther hasn't been well. She's not been behaving with much sense recently, but that doesn't mean she's silly enough to try killing herself,' Fanny said.

'Then why did she write it and where has she gone?' Fausty's hands were entwined in her skirt and she had begun to sob.

'Catherine slept here. She may be hiding something.' Fanny took back the note and ran back down the stairs.

The others were in the drawing-room, Catherine clinging to Patrick's hand, Gobnait still in her nightdress and robe. The uncles, both heavy-eyed from sleep, had joined the group.

'Esther left a note,' Fanny said without preamble. 'You'd better read it, Patrick.'

She thrust it at her brother who disengaged

185

himself from Catherine's clinging hand and took the paper with its scrawled message.

' "Dearest Fanny. Tell them all how sorry I am, but this is all I can do. There's nothing else. E." Where did you get it?'

'It was on the dresser. She must have written it last night.'

'It means—Mother of God, I don't like to think what it means,' Fausty moaned, coming into the drawing-room. 'Sean, Stevie?'

Her anguished gaze had gone to her brothers.

'She'd no cause to do anything silly, had she?' Sean said at last.

'The poor lamb hasn't been well for weeks,' Huldah put in. 'I've had a feeling.'

'Huldah always has feelings *after* something has happened,' Gobnait said.

'We don't know anything has happened at all,' Fanny said harshly. 'Catherine, did you hear nothing at all last night? Did you speak to Esther?'

'She was in bed,' Catherine said, screwing up her face in an effort to remember. 'I said goodnight to her and she said it back. I was so tired that I went straight off to sleep and when I woke up—she'd gone down to breakfast I thought.'

'But why would she write such a note?' Gobnait asked. 'Did she care more about Philip Ashton than we realized?'

'What's Philip Ashton got to do with it?'

186

Patrick asked.

'She was in love with him,' said Gobnait. 'Oh, she didn't say much, but I guessed. They had a quarrel or something. I didn't enquire too deeply because I was busy getting ready for the Show, and I don't believe in prying.'

'We shall have to mount a search,' Patrick broke in. 'There's no point in standing here speculating. She's probably just giving us all a fright.'

His tone was far from confident and the glance he gave Fanny was heavy with questioning.

CHAPTER ELEVEN

'There must be something we can do.' Fausty, her face drawn with the anxiety of a day's waiting, stood by the window, wringing her hands over and over.

'Everything possible is being done,' Fanny soothed. 'She isn't in the immediate district, Patrick and the uncles have searched every nook and cranny. She must be safe, hiding somewhere to frighten us.'

'Esther wouldn't do such a thing,' Fausty said. 'I've never known her do anything spiteful, not even when she was a child.'

'But she is vague,' Fanny said quickly. 'It's likely she's wandered away somewhere.'

'Then someone surely would have seen her,' Fausty said in despair. 'She was in her nightgown!'

'There's an old cloak of Huldah's missing from the back of the kitchen door,' Fanny reminded her. 'And a pair of Esther's shoes, the grey ones with beads on the toes. I can't find them.'

'She must have put on her shoes and snatched up the cloak on her way out,' Fausty said.

'Then perhaps she didn't intend to harm herself,' Fanny said, but even in her own ears her voice carried no conviction.

The note that her sister had left implied its own chilling message. It was a message Fanny's mind refused to accept yet, deep within her, was a tiny spark of dreary triumph. She had, after all, been right to regard Esther as unbalanced. Only a very unbalanced person would make away with herself. Abruptly she said, 'I cannot sit here doing nothing. I'll go for a short drive, I think. Do you wish to come?'

'I'll remain here in case there's news,' Fausty said. 'You go for a drive, dear. Catherine will stay with me, won't you?'

'Yes, of course,' Catherine said promptly.

Fanny took up her cloak and went out. It was a relief to be in the fresh air away from the brooding atmosphere of the house, where every hour that passed brought a corresponding drop in hope.

'Going out?' Patrick asked the unnecessary question as she was mounting into the driving-seat. 'The daylight will be fading soon.'

'Anything is better than sitting around waiting for news,' Fanny said restlessly.

'Move over then and I'll drive you.' He clambered over the wheel and took the reins from her. 'Gobnait rode over to the Grants' to find out if they had heard anything and the uncles went down to the river.'

She stared at him for a moment before his meaning penetrated, then her face paled and she suppressed a cry.

'The men are out with the dragging nets,'

Patrick said flatly. 'I'm sorry, Fan, but they have to start early before the—before anything is swept too far down-river to be retrieved.'

'Let's drive in the other direction,' Fanny said quickly.

'Likely they'll find nothing at all,' Patrick said with determined cheerfulness. 'We'll drive slowly and enjoy the sunshine.'

'Oh, I wish it were possible to enjoy something!' Fanny exclaimed fervently. 'I feel that I shall never be able to enjoy anything ever again.'

'I wish I could start understanding why she left such a note,' her brother said moodily. 'Gobnait has been dropping dark hints about Philip, but he's been away. I did get the idea that he admired Esther but we never got to talking about it. How did Esther feel about him?'

'She didn't say. You know how vague Esther always is.'

'Perhaps Elizabeth will be able to tell Gobnait something. She and Esther are friendly, are they not?'

'I think Esther would have been more inclined to confide in me,' Fanny said. She hesitated a moment before continuing. 'As a matter of fact, from what she said to me, I gained the impression that she had become too fond of Philip. He perhaps realized what was happening and tried to tell her.'

'Philip keeps his own counsel even in his

cups,' Patrick said. 'Is that all you know?'

'Well, I have rather felt—' Again Fanny hesitated.

'Felt what?' He swung the trap round a curve in the road.

'Only that Philip—I believe, that he developed rather a tendresse for me. I have done nothing to encourage him but Esther— she may have guessed or he may have said more than he intended. I can't say anything more definite and I may be mistaken.'

'If Philip Ashton led Esther on and then turned her down,' Patrick said, 'I'll wring his— speak of the devil! Here comes the Ashton carriage.'

'With Lady Ashton inside,' Fanny said, torn between dread and disappointment.

'We'd better stop. She may not have heard.' He tossed the reins into Fanny's lap as he drew up and climbed down into the open road.

The closed carriage had also stopped and Lady Ashton's handsome, high-turbanned head appeared at the window. Patrick had strode towards her and was talking earnestly but the coach was too far away for Fanny to hear the words spoken. She sat in a frenzy of impatience, fiddling with the reins, hopefully nodding and smiling as Lady Ashton glanced in her direction. The woman responded with a bow and a smile, then turned her attention back to Patrick, cupping her hands over her mouth in a fashion that was extremely

191

irritating to the watching girl.

After what seemed an age Patrick stepped away from the window, bowing as the coach rattled past. Lady Ashton had already wound up the window and Fanny had a brief glimpse of her satisfied profile before she leaned back against the leather cushions.

'Had she heard?' Fanny asked anxiously as Patrick reseated himself and took the reins from her.

'She was bound for a dinner engagement in Otley,' he answered.

'But had she heard that Esther is missing?'

He shook his head, his expression so grave that she said impulsively, 'Patrick, what is it? What else did she tell you? For someone who knows nothing she had a great deal to say!'

'She told me that Esther's disappearance had made her thankful that you had had the courage to tell her the truth,' he said slowly.

'Truth about what?' Something had clenched in the pit of her stomach but she strove to speak calmly. 'What can she possibly mean?'

'Why don't you tell me?' he countered.

'I cannot imagine. I am scarcely likely to have had any tête-à-têtes with Lady Ashton, am I?'

'Fanny.' There was a faint warning in his voice.

'What else did she say?' Fanny demanded.

'I think you know.' The warning in his voice

had a heaviness now and there was a thin white line round his mouth. They were signs that he was about to indulge in one of his rare bouts of temper and the knot in her stomach pulled tighter.

'We haven't seen the Ashtons for ages,' she said quickly. 'You know that! I cannot conceive what she could mean but there must be a perfectly logical explanation.'

'Lady Ashton said that Esther's behaviour merely confirmed her in her opinion of my sister's unfortunate condition,' Patrick said.

'What a very unkind thing to say about Esther!' Fanny exclaimed. 'I begin to think that Lady Ashton's own brain has been turned by too much Mediterranean sunshine. Perhaps it's as well that she and Philip are not going to be wed!'

'Fanny, stop it!' They had crested a rise and were bowling down into a narrow valley. As they reached the bottom he drew up so sharply that she was almost jolted out of her seat.

'It's all too ridiculous!' she cried.

'Stop it! Stop babbling!' He put his hand on her shoulder and shook her. 'What did you tell Lady Ashton that made her forbid the marriage between Philip and Esther?'

'What could I possibly have said? You know how snobbish Lady Ashton is. She will not be content with anyone beneath the rank of countess as a wife for—Philip. You're hurting my arm! Please let go.'

'When you've told me the truth, and don't try to look innocent. Large blue eyes may sway other young men, but I'm your brother and they're wasted on me. You went to see Lady Ashton.'

'To enquire after Henry. He'd caught a cold.'

'You're not engaged to him, are you?'

'No. He did ask me, but I decided against it.'

'So why did you visit the Ashtons'? Was it to inform Lady Ashton that Esther was unbalanced? Was it to break up some understanding between her and Philip?'

'You've no right to question me so!' Her temper flared to match his. 'I want to go home now. Turn about so that we can go home!'

'First you'll tell me what you told Lady Ashton about Esther. Did you tell her Esther is unbalanced? How could you lie so?'

'It wasn't a lie! She is unbalanced! You never see it because you're scarcely ever at home. You don't have to clear up her mess when she leaves a task half done or try to remind her of what she intended to do and promptly forgot! You don't understand. Esther isn't fit to be wed to anyone. She's exactly like Aunt Dotty!'

Her voice rose shrilly and the faint echo of it was flung back by the surrounding slopes.

'Aunt Dotty died when we were little,' Patrick interrupted.

194

'And she wasn't right in the head! Mother was always jesting about her bad memory and the way she used to muddle up people's names!'

'And the fact that Mother did jest is proof positive that there was nothing really wrong with Aunt Dotty,' he said. 'Mother would never laugh at anyone who was truly afflicted. Aunt Dotty was vague and a mite eccentric. Maiden ladies sometimes get that way but there was nothing wrong with her sanity, and there's nothing wrong with Esther's sanity either.'

'She's too delicate for marriage.'

'Since when did they make you a doctor?' he demanded roughly. 'If Philip wished to marry her—is that why he went away? There's a rumour that he quarrelled with his family. Was it about Esther?'

'They would never have suited! Philip is too much under his mother's domination for a gentle soul like Esther. He needs a strong-minded, vigorous girl.'

'Like you, I suppose?' Staring at her he began to laugh without mirth. 'That's it, isn't it? You set your cap at Philip Ashton and he'd have none of you. He wanted to marry Esther, so you went to Lady Ashton with your poisonous little tale and she believed it. I suppose your next move would have been to offer sympathy and consolation and persuade Lady Ashton that you are as sensible as Esther is crazy?'

'I love Philip!' Fanny's face was anguished as she stared at him. 'I love him, don't you understand? Esther could never make a suitable mistress of Ashton House! The marriage would have been a disaster from the start.'

'How much does Esther know? You didn't tell her!'

'Of course not,' Fanny said indignantly. 'All that Esther knows is that Lady Ashton forbade the match. I don't know what passed between Philip and his mother, save that there was a quarrel. I meant only what was best for poor Esther.'

'And now there are men dragging the river for her,' he said tightly. 'Is that better than her being wed to Philip? Is it?'

'No, of course not. But they wouldn't have been happy together.'

'And you and he would, I suppose? Well, that's one service I can render Esther whether she's alive or dead!'

'What are you talking about? You wouldn't tell—I truly believed! I truly believed that Esther was like Aunt Dotty.'

'You truly believed you could steal Philip from Esther,' Patrick contradicted. 'Oh, perhaps you didn't think out the harm you could cause, but that's no excuse! So we'll drive over to Ashton House right now and you can tell Sir John what you just told me! He has not attended the evening engagement for which his lady wife was bound.'

'I'll not come,' she began, but he overrode her with a passion of which she had not believed him capable.

'You've no choice! You'll tell Sir John and anyone else who happens to be there exactly how much mischief you've wrought.'

'What good will that do poor Esther now?' Fanny cried.

'Probably none, but at least it will prevent your snaring Philip.'

He shook off her restraining hand and slapped the whip across Belle's flanks with such ferocity that the pony bounded forward, the wheels of the trap rattling over rough ground, the trap itself tilting. For an instance both Patrick and Fanny were off balance and in that instant, without coherent thought or plan, she hit out with all her strength. Her brother, intent on controlling the pony, had no chance of regaining his balance. He fell, the reins slipping through his hands, the wheel catching his leg with a force that, judging from his cry of pain, must surely have broken it.

She grabbed at the dangling rein and pulled Belle's head to the left, describing a wide circle that brought the vehicle round in the opposite direction. Patrick was struggling up on his elbow, but she was unable to discern his features clearly through the red mist that filled her eyes and there was no room for any

197

thought in her mind but the fact that Philip might be lost to her for ever if the truth came out.

The whip was gone but she raised her voice in an incoherent shout and the normally placid Belle, confused and alarmed, plunged ahead. The trap buckled and tipped, the wheels spinning helplessly, and Fanny had an impression of earth and sky revolving. She landed on turf and lay for a moment, winded by the fall. There had been a rending of wood and metal that seemed to pierce through to her brain but the silence that followed was even more frightening.

In falling her bonnet had slipped and was perched drunkenly over her ear and her ribs hurt when she gingerly touched them. She scrambled to her feet, tugging off the bonnet and uttering a sharp cry of pain as one of her curls became entangled with the dangling ribbon. Her vision was clearing but she felt weak and breathless.

Belle stood, head drooping and sides heaving between the broken shafts of the trap and beneath the wheels a red stain dyed the ground faster than the approaching sunset. Fanny approached on shaking legs. What lay beneath the overturned vehicle was no longer living, only a tangle of arms and legs with head bent back at an unnatural angle.

'I didn't mean it, Patrick. It was an accident. I truly didn't mean it.'

198

She didn't realize she had spoken aloud until she heard her own voice in the stillness. Her side hurt when she drew a deep breath and she was cold.

There was no house near. She ought to unhitch Belle and ride the pony home but her fingers felt stiff and clumsy when she tried to loosen the straps. She patted Belle absently and walked, without conscious thought, up the slope. If she paused and looked back, down into the shallow valley, the hideous scene would have vanished like a dream. The prospect of that was so real that, when she did turn and look, it was an almost physical shock to see the overturned trap, the bloodied figure pinned beneath, the pony still trembling with ears laid back and flaring nostrils.

There was something else. A burly figure had appeared on the crest of the further rise and was hurrying down to the wreckage. She recognized the figure before she heard the hoarse shout. Joe Wilton, weaving home on foot after a prolonged drinking bout, had come upon the scene. His arrival invested the situation with an added horror. Without waiting to discover if he had noticed her, Fanny turned and fled down the slope. It hurt to run but fear spurred her against the pain of bruised ribs. That thick-set figure, silhouetted against the rising dark, had terrified her. The memory still terrified her as she ran, stumbling over the torn hem of her skirt, her breath sobbing in her throat. She fell once, grazing her wrists and the palms of her hands. Somewhere in the nightmare of incidents that had made up the whole catastrophe she must have lost her gloves as well as her bonnet. It was of small importance now but she heard herself giving little, gasping moans as she scrambled up and ran on, swerving wildly over the curving track as it dipped between heather-clad turf.

She could see the dark mass of Sabre Hall standing against the sunset, but her feet were weighted with lead and her side felt as if it were on fire. She concentrated on placing one foot before another while the outlines of the house wavered and shimmered before her eyes and her own harsh breathing mingled with the hoofbeats that approached.

'Mother of God, what's happened? Have you found Esther?'

Fanny leaned weakly against the side of her uncle's horse as he dismounted and put an arm around her.

'Sean! Sean, will you come over here?' He raised his voice to the other approaching rider.

'What happened?' Sean was demanding in his turn. 'Fanny, darling, has someone attacked you?'

'Attacked?' Her voice broke on a note of hysteria.

'Give her a drop of brandy,' Stephen commanded, tugging a flask out of the pocket of his greatcoat.

The first gulp made her head spin and her eyes water. She pushed the flask away from her chattering teeth and stood straighter.

'Esther? You've not found her?' she managed to articulate.

'Neither hair nor hide. Fanny darling, what put you into this sorry state?'

'Attacked,' she repeated.

'Who attacked you? Who?' Sean was demanding.

'Wilton. Joe Wilton,' she began.

'And who is Joe Wilton when he's at home?' Stephen interjected.

'Isn't he the fellow in charge down at the mill?' Sean asked.

'Was in charge! Patrick dismissed—'

'And where the devil is Patrick? He was going to join us down at the river,' Stephen asked.

'Dead.' She spoke flatly, her eyes moving from one startled face to the other.

'Dead? Girl, what are you saying?' Stephen took his arm from about her shoulders and gaped at her.

'Fanny, what are you saying?' Sean exclaimed.

'Patrick's dead,' she said and began to shake again from head to foot. 'He's dead. Joe Wilton came and I—'

'Was it Wilton killed him?'

'Killed him?' She hesitated, her mind still

held in the grip of recent horror, then heard her own voice running on. 'Yes, he was there, you see that don't you? He was on his way to Sabre Hall, to ask for his job back. There was a fight. There was a terrible fight. I ran. I ran so fast. It was Wilton.'

'I'll go and find out what's been going on,' Stephen said. 'Get the poor child back into the house.'

'He's dead,' Fanny said again. 'My brother is dead. Patrick is dead.'

If she went on saying it in every possible way then she might begin to believe what was happening.

'Come on, darling.' The voice interrupted her and she was lifted to the saddle where she clung, still trembling, tears falling unheeded down her cheeks.

Life became a series of disconnected incidents. Her mother stood in the hall, eyes enormous, her hands still wringing together in the folds of her skirt. She was questioning her brother in a tongue that Fanny couldn't understand. Some remnant of common sense told the girl that it must be the Gaelic to which Fausty had reverted in a moment of stress.

Huldah was crying. Fanny couldn't remember ever having seen Huldah cry. Catherine was crying too in little, gulping sobs, her mouth squaring like a child's, her soft, brown hair hanging loosely about her neck in a way that made Fanny think of Esther.

Gobnait was not weeping. Her face was a carved mask of fury and she was walking rapidly up and down the drawing-room, kicking her unfashionably trailing skirt aside every time she turned.

There were other feet trampling through the house, other voices raised in question and command. Fanny lay with a rug over her on the couch in the lamplit parlour and drank hot soup. She had glimpsed a shrouded form being carried past the door but the door was closed now and a constable—she couldn't recall his name though he had given it—had drawn up a low chair and sat with notebook open and pencil poised.

'Take your time, Miss Sabre. No need to rush anything,' he was saying.

'It must be very late.' She pushed back her hair and sat up.

'Past midnight, Miss. Not to worry. I was out at Otley visiting my aunt when word came. If you could just tell me what's happened and I can take it down.'

'My brother and I went for a drive. We needed some air, some time to discuss what might have happened to Esther. You know that my sister is missing?'

'Yes, Miss. No doubt we'll find her,' he returned stolidly.

'We were talking, wondering what might have happened to her,' Fanny hurried on. 'Then we saw Joe Wilton.'

'Your overseer,' the constable nodded.

'My brother, Patrick, had dismissed him. This morning.' She spoke with an air of surprise. It was hard to realize that so much had happened since she had woken that morning.

'For what reason, Miss?'

'Wilton got exceedingly drunk at the Horse Show yesterday and insulted me,' she explained. 'It was not the first time. He was frequently very rude and had been warned about it. This morning I drove to the mill. Wilton had gone in to work as usual though he had been told only to collect the wages due to him. He was most abusive. He pulled me from the trap—actually pulled me from the trap. Patrick knocked him down for it. Thomas Leigh, our clerk, came out from the counting-house and saw it all. Patrick drove me home again.'

'What did Wilton do?'

'He uttered threats. I cannot remember his exact words. I thought—Patrick didn't take them seriously.'

'And then you met Joe Wilton this evening—last evening.' He glanced at the clock.

'We drove out to talk. Patrick stopped to speak to Wilton when we met him. There was an argument.'

'About the loss of his job?'

'He wanted to return. Patrick wouldn't

agree. They were arguing and then Wilton reached up and dragged Patrick from the driving-seat. He—Wilton I mean—was beating my brother about the head and the pony was bucking and rearing. I must have been flung clear as Belle, that's the pony, wheeled about and the trap was upset. I saw Wilton push Patrick right into its path and then I started running. I don't know how I managed to run.'

'What did Wilton do?' the constable enquired.

'I didn't stop to see.' Fanny lifted her hands, then let them fall into her lap again. 'I ran and ran until I met my uncles. I ought to have stayed to help Patrick, but I was so frightened that I just ran. I shall never forgive myself for that.'

Tears had welled up into her eyes again and she groped for a handkerchief.

'Your brother was past help, Miss,' the constable said. 'His skull was crushed by the wheel. There was nothing you could have done for him.'

'It was Wilton. I saw Wilton push him,' she repeated.

'That makes it murder,' the constable said heavily. 'The rest of it might have been a fight and Mr Sabre's death not intended. Manslaughter they call it in law. But the push—that makes it murder.'

'The man is a brute, a dangerous brute.' The girl shivered, pulling the rug higher.

'He'll do no more harm. He was picked up by some of your mill-hands when he was fleeing from the scene.'

'Picked up? What did he say?'

'Denies it, of course. Said he'd been drinking—not that he needed to say so. The ale was strong on his breath.'

'But what did he say?'

'Only that he'd found Mr Sabre trapped beneath the wheel. He'd seen he was dead and claims he was running for help. He'd lamed his own mount earlier, says he'd ridden her too hard, which explains why he was on foot. There were cuts on his face.'

'I told you they fought this morning. Patrick horsewhipped him for the violence he'd shown towards me. I told you.'

'And very clearly, Miss, considering your state of shock. I shall have to write this up as a statement and get you to sign it in the morning when you've had a good night's sleep.'

'My sister—there's no word, I suppose?'

The man shook. his head, snapping his notebook shut. 'It seems the young lady went of her own accord. We'll probably mount a full search for her at dawn, but for now I don't think there's much I can do.'

'My mother will be heart-broken,' Fanny said.

'She's resting now. Your other sister, Miss Gobnait, is with her.'

'My uncles—?'

'On their way to York with a letter from me to the magistrate and Joe Wilton prisoner between them. Some of the mill-hands were for hanging him at once, but the law must be upheld. He'll be tried at the Assizes in the spring.'

'Shall I have to go?' she asked fearfully.

'To give evidence? Your statement might be sufficient, though Wilton will be entitled to Counsel and Counsel might want to question you, but there's nothing to be nervous about,' he reassured. 'Lady witnesses are given every consideration.'

'You've been very kind.' Fanny pushed aside the rug and put her feet to the floor. 'Have you been offered food—a bed?'

'Both, Miss Sabre, thank you kindly. I'll get this statement written up and you can put your name on it in the morning. Your housekeeper said she'd sent for a doctor to look you over but you don't seem to be badly hurt.'

'I might have been dead. Wilton might have killed me too!'

'You're a fortunate young lady, though you might not think so at this moment. However, you've nothing more to fear from Joe Wilton.'

'Thank you.' She rose, holding onto the arm of the couch as dizziness threatened to overwhelm her again.

'I'm sorry, very sorry about your brother,' the constable said. 'Very sorry indeed, Miss Sabre. I didn't know the young gentleman personally, but I understand he will be a great loss to the neighbourhood.'

'Thank you,' Fanny repeated and made her way hastily to the door before tears overwhelmed her again.

CHAPTER TWELVE

It had been a most dignified funeral. There had been nothing in the sombre ceremony to remind any of the mourners who thronged the churchyard that Patrick Sabre had been half-Irish by blood and almost wholly Irish by temperament. Instead there had been a tasteful eulogy to remind everybody that a young and promising life had been cut short by violence and that the one accused of the crime was now behind bars. The first handful of earth had been scattered on the coffin and Catherine had given a little sigh and fainted clean away.

There would be no funeral tea and there was no will to read and be quarrelled over. Patrick had been due to come into full ownership of house and mill only after Fausty's death. Now it would be Gobnait who would inherit both, and Gobnait took as little interest in the business as her brother had done. Certainly she would not interfere with Fanny's plans.

'A sad day, Miss Sabre.' The vicar shook hands gravely, glancing over to the coach where Catherine was being revived with hartshorn and vinegar.

'Very sad.' Fanny compressed her lips to check an involuntary sob.

'And a terrible experience for you. We can only be thankful that you were not seriously injured when that ruffian sprang upon you.'

'I try not to think about it,' she said shuddering.

She had gone over the story so often in the three days between death and burial that it was as real to her as if it had actually happened. She could almost see Joe Wilton pulling her brother from the trap and then deliberately shoving him into the path of the oncoming horse.

'There is something,' she remembered. 'Wilton had a wife and children.'

'Unhappy creatures!' The vicar shook his head.

'There is no need for them to be thrown on the parish,' Fanny said. 'Will you tell her she is welcome to stay in her own cottage and there will be work in the mill for the older children?'

'That is truly Christian of you, Miss Sabre!' he exclaimed.

'It is what my poor brother would have wished,' she said sadly.

The dead were buried and would be weighted down in spring when the ground had settled, by a tastefully inscribed marble headstone. There remained the problem of Esther. The search was still continuing but in a desultory manner. Nobody spoke of the possibility of her being found alive and the probability of her death had been tacitly assumed. The not knowing was the worst part of all. One could mourn for Patrick but Esther had vanished like a shadow. The awful insidious thing was that Catherine seemed unconsciously to have stepped into her shoes. She slept still in Esther's room, littered with Esther's things, spoke gently and moved softly as Esther had done, and was in a fair way to becoming an echo of the missing girl. She also wept a great deal. No doubt she had taken Patrick's attentions seriously. Certainly she showed no interest in the thought of any other young men and she had not mentioned her eventual return to Ireland.

It was, surprisingly, Stephen who brought up the matter the day after the funeral. He came into the parlour where Fanny was replying to letters of condolence and began without preamble.

'If you've a minute to spare I'll take a word.'

'Of course, Uncle.' She laid down her pen and gave him her attention.

'You don't like me much, do you?' he began, and held up a hand as she opened her mouth. 'Now don't be bothering to deny it! You give me one of your faint cool smiles and I can read your wishes clear as if you'd written them down. We're not good enough, Sean and I, for your fine and fancy notions. And we're Irish, which is a bigger crime in your eyes. Well, it was fine here while we had Patrick's company but he's gone now and the autumn's coming on and we've the mood on us to sail home again.'

'I thought you planned to stay at least until after Christmas,' she said in surprise.

'Well, we've changed our minds and it's not a bit of use trying to make out you're sorry,' he said cheerfully. 'Sean and I will be off at the end of the week, but Catherine's taken a fancy to stay on here. You'd not be objecting to that?'

'Of course not. Catherine is a sweet girl and we've grown very fond of her,' she said.

'And you'll treat her right, see that she gets to meet young men?'

'As soon as our period of mourning is over,' Fanny said. 'Catherine, being cousin to Patrick, will be able to accept social invitations again after Christmas. But Esther is not yet found.'

'And may never be.' Stephen shrugged and gave her a wry look. 'The truth is that this place gets on my nerves. Sean's too. We're neither fish nor fowl here, so it's best we go back but Catherine likes the neighbourhood and she's a fancy to become a lady.'

'I'm sure we shall be glad to have her stay on,' Fanny said cordially, 'but ought you not to consult Mother?'

'Everyone knows who the real mistress is,' he returned. 'Young Gobnait's only interest is in the stables and Fausty's still grieving too hard to take any notice of anything. The heart is gone out of her.'

'It went out of her when my father died.

That was the great tragedy of her life,' Fanny said softly.

'Ah, that's as may be. She never talks of him,' he said.

'Because it is too painful for her. He was a very fine man.'

'As you say.' He sketched her a salute that struck her as unsuitably frivolous under the circumstances and went out.

Sighing, she turned again to the pile of letters. There were more than forty of them, delivered that morning, and tied up in a neat packet. She had not realized how popular her brother had been nor how wide was his circle of friends. There was even a brief, cold note with the Ashton crest on it. Lady Ashton evidently regarded being murdered as inexcusable carelessness.

Fanny set the letter aside to be answered later and ruffled through the rest. Only about half of them had been franked. Huldah had paid the postage due on the rest, grumbling that she saw no reason why one should pay out good brass for reading the same thing over and over.

Esther's round, childish handwriting leapt up at her from one of the franked letters. Fanny stared at it for a full minute while there rushed through her a variety of emotions ranging from blank shock to the wildest hope. If Esther had written then there was a strong possibility that she was still alive, that she had given up any idea of killing herself. Fingers shaking, she broke the seal and folded out the missive.

'Dearest Fanny,

'I'm writing to you because I know you will choose the right moment to tell the others. The day you all went to the Show I slipped out to meet Philip. We made hurried plans then, but I had to wait until everybody was asleep before I could steal away. I was unable even to put on a dress because Catherine began to stir, so I left in my nightgown with only an old cloak thrown about me, which is very shocking but there was no help for it.

'Philip and I went by hired gig to Hull and were married by special licence there the next day. He will be cut off by his family but he cares nothing for them, not since his mother invented terrible lies about me to try to stop the marriage. He will not say exactly what they were for fear of upsetting me. In all things he is most considerate.

'We are going to travel on the Continent for a year or two. Philip has an allowance he inherited from his grandmother which his parents cannot touch so you need not fret about our being in want. I know you will wish us happy, my dearest sister. Write to me care of the British Consul in Florence. We shall go there first for Philip says of all

214

cities Florence is the one where honeymoons should be spent.

    'Your loving sister,

    'Esther Sabre Ashton.'

Esther alive and wed to Philip. Esther, unaware of Patrick's death and on her way to winter in Italy. Fanny had to read the letter over twice before its full meaning sank in and even then the words slid off the surface of her mind. *Esther alive and wed to Philip.*

'But she left a note,' Fanny said aloud. 'She left a suicide note.'

But that first note had not been explicit. It might have meant anything. 'Tell them all how sorry I am, but this is all I can do. There's nothing else.' Nothing else but to shame her entire family by eloping—and in her nightgown! Lady Ashton would never forgive Philip and Philip would never be able to return. And there had been no real need for Patrick to die since, with Philip and Esther married, it would have made no difference what he chose to tell the Ashtons. Patrick was dead and she had lost Philip for ever. Fanny sat motionless for a moment longer, then leapt up with an incoherent cry, sweeping letters and writing materials off the table onto the carpet.

'Fanny, what is it? What's wrong?' Fausty, her expression startled, hurried in from the hall with one of her brothers at her heels.

'Esther! Esther is—'

'Dead?' Fausty put both hands to her mouth.

'Married!' Fanny bent, scrabbled for the letter, and thrust it at her mother. 'She never killed herself at all! She never even meant to kill herself! She ran off in her nightgown and married Philip Ashton!'

'Thanks be to God,' Fausty said shakily.

'She's disgraced us!' Fanny's voice was shrill and she could no longer conceal her shaking. 'She eloped with Philip Ashton. All these days when we've been searching for her and worried out of our minds she's been gallivanting all over the county getting herself wed.'

'Read the letter to me, Sean. I'm all of a quiver,' Fausty said.

'They've gone to Italy!' Fanny snatched back the letter and pointed to the offending sentence. 'They've sailed to Florence where we may write to them, care of the Consul, she kindly invites! No word of regret for the trouble she's caused. Mother, she is the most selfish creature alive!'

'But she is alive,' Fausty said. 'I had accepted the fact that she was dead but she's alive, Fanny.'

'And Patrick is dead,' Fanny said. 'Patrick is dead and it is all Esther's fault!'

'How in the name of all that's holy do you reach that conclusion?' Sean enquired.

'Because,' she hesitated, then rushed on.

'Because Patrick and I would not have been driving out on the moor if Esther had not been missing in the first place! He would still be alive, don't you see? I will never forgive her for that, and I will never agree to receive either of them in this house!'

Sobbing, she fled upstairs, leaving her mother and her uncle to stare after her in consternation.

Catherine, pale in her mourning dress, appeared at the door of Esther's room, anxiously enquiring what was wrong.

'Esther is married to Philip Ashton.' Fanny choked, pushing past her into the bedroom. 'She is not dead at all.'

'But that's wonderful, Cousin. Don't you think that's wonderful?' Catherine stammered.

'Wonderful! The Ashtons threatened to disinherit Philip if he married Esther and they will keep their word, but she cares only for getting her own way in all things. She was always like that from a child! Selfish to the bone! I covered up for her over and over again to save my good mother pain and because I was fond of my sister. Sister! She is no longer my sister!'

'Oh, Fanny,' Catherine began helplessly, but the other girl whirled about, her face scarlet, her voice rasping.

'I mean it, Catherine! We all thought that Esther had killed herself. So, as far as I'm concerned, she is dead! I no longer have a twin sister, I no longer have one.'

She turned and began to pile up the clutter of ribbons and flowers that were strewn over the dresser, her lips and hands moving with a fevered energy. Catherine was gazing at her in horror. There were flying footsteps along the gallery and Gobnait burst in, her vivid hair escaping from its pins.

'Is it true? I heard Mother saying that Esther is alive.'

'And wed to Philip Ashton,' Fanny retorted. 'His parents have disinherited him.'

'More fools they!' Gobnait tossed her head scornfully. 'No doubt they'd reasons for forbidding the match! Thinking themselves better than the rest of us, I don't doubt. And Philip defied them? I didn't know he had so much spirit!'

'It was a dreadful thing to do,' Fanny said, her hands shredding a length of ribbon. 'She has disgraced us.'

'By running away to be married? I never guessed that Esther had so much spirit either,' Gobnait grinned.

'Nobody will receive them,' Fanny said tensely. 'They have offended against every convention. To go without any word but a note that led us to believe she was making away with herself. That was cruel.'

'I don't suppose Esther imagined we'd draw that conclusion.'

'Esther has no imagination. She never did

have any imagination! All she ever had was a determination to get her own way regardless of what it might cost anyone else. I shall never forgive her, nor allow her to set foot here again.'

'As to that.' Gobnait paused, her expression thoughtful as she stared at the younger girl. Then she lifted one thin shoulder with an elegant shrug and said, 'Of course you must do as you please but I daresay Mother will be happy to know she's still alive.'

'Will you write to her?' Catherine asked when Gobnait had left the room.

'I'll pack up her belongings and send them on to her,' Fanny said. 'I'll not send any letter. Mother is bound to write and let her know about Patrick—oh, Catherine, pray don't begin to weep again.'

'I cannot help it.' Catherine dabbed at her eyes with an inadequate scrap of linen. 'This has been such a terrible week! I was so happy a few days ago after Patrick asked me to wed him.'

'Asked you to what?' The frayed ribbon uncurled itself from Fanny's hand and trailed limply on the table.

'He wanted me to marry him,' the other confided. 'He said it was time for him to settle down and take an interest in the mill. He asked me to be his wife. We were going to tell everybody and then poor Esther seemed so unhappy we decided it would be kinder to wait until she was feeling better.'

'Patrick wanted to marry you?'

'But we never did announce it,' Catherine said mournfully. 'It was such a lovely secret between the two of us and now it's all ended and Patrick is dead.'

'I thought you wanted to stay in England so that you could find a husband,' Fanny said blankly.

'I told the uncles that.' Catherine stopped weeping and blushed. 'They don't like it in England but they're ready to have me stay here.'

'But Patrick is dead,' Fanny said, her brain whirling. 'Are you hoping to find another husband?'

'I shall never marry,' Catherine said sadly. 'I shall never marry and I shall never go back to Ireland. If my parents knew—' She paused, her eyes pleading.

'I don't quite understand,' Fanny said. 'Surely your parents could not have objected to your marrying Patrick? I thought that he was fond of—well, it doesn't matter now. He and Elizabeth had been friends from childhood and it was rather expected. However, that's all past!'

'Don't you want me to stay?' Catherine's lip trembled violently.

'Of course I do,' Fanny said warmly. 'I have grown very fond of you, Cousin. We have all grown fond of you and I would have been very pleased if you and my brother had decided to marry.' With no possibility of such an event ever happening now she could say that with every appearance of sincerity.

'But I cannot go home,' Catherine said. 'Oh, Fanny, don't be angry with me please. I know we behaved badly but Patrick was going to marry me. He fell in love with me the first moment we met.'

'You're with child,' Fanny said, and sat down heavily on the nearest stool.

'It's too soon to tell.' Catherine knelt impulsively, taking her cousin's hand in both her own. 'It's less than a month since we— since he—'

'Seduced you,' Fanny said flatly.

'He loved me,' Catherine said eagerly. 'He was going to wed me but we were too impatient to wait. My parents will never forgive me if they find out.'

'But you cannot keep it from them for ever!'

'I am not certain yet,' Catherine said, 'for I never was with child before. But I have been sick twice this week and my curse hasn't come. In a few months I shall begin to show.'

'But your mother and father will have to know,' Fanny repeated.

'I thought I could stay here until after I'd had the babe and then go home,' Catherine said earnestly. 'I could leave it with you and Aunt Fausty if you like. I wouldn't know how to look after a baby and Patrick—he would want his child to be brought up here. Only the uncles mustn't know. They were supposed to look after me.'

'They don't seem to have been very efficient at it,' Fanny said dryly.

Her first shock was fading and the glance she bent upon her cousin was almost loving. Patrick, for all his careless ways, would never seriously have considered taking his little, provincial cousin as his bride and the future mistress of Sabre Hall had he not believed that it was his duty if she proved to be with child. At least there had been that much honour in him. His death had been less of a disaster than his marriage to Catherine would have been.

'You won't say anything until after the uncles have gone back, will you?' Catherine begged.

'We won't say a word until we are certain one way or the other,' Fanny reassured her.

'And you're not angry? You always behave so correctly that I feared you'd be very angry,' Catherine said. 'Why, Esther is legally wed and you won't have her in the house.'

'That's a different affair,' Fanny said. 'Esther was my sister and I expected a different standard of behaviour from her. She ought to have confided in me.'

'I know I was never a lady,' Catherine said humbly, 'but my parents were always very strict with me. At home it's a terrible disgrace to bear a bastard.'

222

'It is not exactly smiled upon here,' Fanny said in the same dry tone. All her emotions had drained away and there was nothing left in her but an aching weariness.

'You can have the babe,' Catherine said.

She had known the intimate embrace of the man she loved and now she talked about giving away the fruit of that embrace as if it were no more than a doll. Fanny drew her hands away gently and rose.

'We'll come to some arrangement when matters are more settled,' she said. 'Patrick behaved very badly but he intended to wed you. It will be good to have something of his to remember him by. Now, dry your eyes and start to pack up Esther's things. This is your room now.'

If she stayed any longer she too would begin to weep. Too much was happening too swiftly and she felt weakly confused.

Esther had stolen Philip, and Patrick had seduced his cousin with a promise of marriage that he had surely never intended. Two events, both marked with dishonour, she rejected bitterly. She had lost Philip and her brother was dead because of that terrible Wilton. She had only to close her eyes to visualize the thick-set figure pushing the younger man into the path of the oncoming horse. In a few months, when Wilton had been safely hanged, she would find it easy to forget that anything different ever happened.

There was a different atmosphere in the house. Fanny was aware of it the moment she walked downstairs. Gobnait's excited voice echoed from the kitchen where, no doubt, she was imparting the news to Huldah. The sunlight of early autumn flooded the hall as if it were a new springtime. Everybody was glad that Esther was alive, everybody except herself. She could feel no gladness at all. There was nothing in her but a cold, heavy disappointment that gripped her like a sickness. It had all gone wrong. By this time Philip and she ought to have been engaged and Esther preparing to marry Henry with Patrick and Gobnait matched neatly with the Grants. Instead Patrick was dead and Esther disgraced and her own heart broken.

From the parlour she heard her mother's voice, raised in the Gaelic she spoke privately with her brothers. It merely served to emphasize the isolation in which Fanny felt herself to stand.

She turned abruptly and went into the dining-room. Here, at least, was a measure of peace and permanence, the carved, dark furniture reflecting in its polished surface the few pieces of silver and copper ranged about the room, the portrait of her father in its accustomed place. She went to stand beneath it, raising her eyes to the handsome face with its frame of dark red hair.

From behind her Fausty said tentatively,

224

'Fanny, are you all right?'

'I was just thinking,' Fanny said bitterly, not turning, 'that for the first time I am glad that father didn't live. He was such a great gentleman that Esther's conduct would have shamed him to the heart.'

'You think so?' Fausty came to stand at her side, raising her own eyes to the picture.

'I think I know how my own father would have felt,' the girl said reproachfully.

'You never knew him.'

'But I know about him!' Fanny's voice was fierce. 'Earl Sabre, master of Sabre Hall. How would he have felt to learn that his daughter had run away to make a clandestine marriage?'

'He would not have cared much one way or the other,' Fausty said.

'Mother, you can't possibly mean that!' Fanny's eyes flashed from the painted eyes of the portrait to her mother's face. 'Father was a gentleman and he died a hero, trying to rescue Great Aunt Sassie from the fire in the barn!'

'Yes, in that at least he was heroic,' Fausty admitted. 'And he was what most people might call a gentleman.'

'Well then!'

'With no heart and no spirit,' Fausty continued. 'It was all his fault. His father was a hard relentless man who used his purse strings in order to keep his relatives dangling. Earl hated him and hated it here while he was alive but he never broke away. That would have

225

meant standing up to the old man, risking his inheritance. Earl never cared about anything or anyone sufficiently to do that.'

'He married you!'

'And I'm not a lady? That's true. He was fond of me too in his way but he didn't wed me until his father was safely buried and he had Sabre Hall and the mill in his pocket. Oh, it's a long story and I'm not going into it now. He married me but he was always a mite ashamed of me, you see?'

'No. No, I don't see.'

'You won't see,' Fausty said, 'and that's my fault, bringing you up thinking the sun shone out of him! Fanny, he was never a bad man. There's a strength in real badness that can make a man great even if it's in the wrong way. Earl wasn't great in any way at all. He was very charming and he could be kind if it didn't cost him too much effort, but he was idle and feckless and he lost interest in things very speedily. He lost interest in me. I stopped being a person to him very soon and became the woman who could bear him children because he could play with them and spoil them and hand them back to me or Huldah if their demands became too great.'

'I won't listen to this,' Fanny said in a stifled voice. 'I won't listen to any of this.'

'Fanny, darling, think of Patrick! He was his father all over again. I saw it in him.'

'Now you'll traduce your own son,' the girl

226

interrupted. 'I don't understand you, Mother, I don't understand why you're doing this!'

'I thought it was time you learned the truth,' Fausty said, 'but you're not ready for it yet. You're too young to see people as they are and not as you like them to be.'

'It's Esther, isn't it?' Fanny whirled about. 'You think that if you can make me believe bad things about Father then I'll be more inclined to overlook what Esther has done. It won't work, Mother! This may be your house but if she ever entered it again I'd leave it for good! If Esther hadn't run away Patrick might still be alive. I'll always believe that, just as I'll always believe that Father was a brave and gallant gentleman, and nothing you say will ever make me change my opinion!'

She hurried out, banging the door violently behind her.

Fausty drew a long breath, gripping her hands painfully together. Every nerve in her body ached to follow her daughter, to make the girl understand that the world didn't come to an end when the people she tried to mould into her own image of them insisted on behaving as their true natures compelled. Fanny was still very much a child, fierce in her hatreds and her loyalties, seeing everything in black and white. The truth was that she needed a husband who would keep her in check without quelling the lively enthusiasm with which she entered into each fresh endeavour.

Fausty's brown eyes were lifted again to the portrait. Earl gazed back with the same charming indifference he had displayed towards her when he was alive. Patrick had been so much like him that his death had been like losing Earl all over again. Old pain she had fancied long healed had slashed at her heart. She sighed, consciously straightening her shoulders. Earl and Patrick, with all their weakness, were dead. Only the Sabre women were left now and life had to go on.

EPILOGUE

Fanny was on her way back from the mill, the profits from her most recent excursion to market safely accounted in the ledgers. She would be glad when Thomas Leigh finally agreed to retire but the old man was still being obstinate and her mother refused to force his resignation. Such a minor irritation mattered little on such a glorious summer day, however, and she was able to put it to the back of her mind and, with reins slack between her hands, enjoy the beauty of the afternoon as Belle ambled along the track.

It was a pity that her dress didn't match her surroundings but cast a sombre note amid the green and lilac and gold of the moors, but it was less than four months since Catherine had died in childbirth and so mourning was still necessary. At least black suited her rosy complexion and enhanced her red-gold curls and brilliant blue eyes. If Philip Ashton were to ride towards her at this moment he would be certain to fall in love with her. But Philip would never ride into her life now. He and Esther were still in Italy and, though Fausty occasionally received a letter, Fanny never asked to read it nor mentioned her sister's name. There was no communication at all with the Ashtons beyond a cold bow on the rare

229

occasions when they met at church or on some other social occasion. No doubt Lady Ashton believed that the Sabres condoned their son's elopement.

There was someone riding across the moor. Fanny was jerked out of her musing by a momentary glimpse of black hair as the gentleman raised his head but the newcomer was not Philip. He was not anyone she knew, though there was something teasingly familiar about the lean, dark features.

'May I help you?' She drew rein, smiling up at him from beneath the brim of her black straw bonnet.

'I'm not sure, Miss. I'm looking for a lady, a Mrs Sabre,' he answered.

'Oh?' Fanny's fingers tightened the reins as the memory of where she had seen him before flooded back.

'I met the lady a year ago,' he was explaining, 'at the Horse Show in York. It was a fleeting occasion and I've no reason to suppose she recalls me but, as I find myself in this neighbourhood again, I thought I would pay my respects.'

He was younger than her mother, a good ten years younger. In the refreshment tent Fausty had been laughing and talking and the years had rolled away from her.

'I'm told she lives in this district,' he was continuing, puzzled no doubt by her silence. 'As I return to London in a day or two—'

'Lived,' Fanny interposed.

'Lived? You mean she—'

'As you see I am in mourning. Forgive me, but I really must get on, and I wouldn't want you to have a wasted journey,' she said gently.

'I had no idea!' There was a shocked regret in his face. 'My informant assured me.'

'Your information is out of date. We live secluded and news travels very slowly.'

'I'm truly sorry. She was a most charming lady.' He looked embarrassed and awkward as he clutched his hat off.

'She was. Good-day, sir.'

She flicked Belle with the whip and set off at a brisker pace, leaving the man staring after her. Pray God he didn't take it into his head to follow and offer formal condolences! At a bend in the track she glanced back and saw with relief that he was already riding away.

The dark mass of Sabre Hall with its unfenced sweep of turf calmed her spirits. The presumption of the unknown young man in seeking out her mother even made her smile a little. Fausty would be immensely flattered if ever she were told. Fanny had no intention of telling her.

She drove the trap expertly into the courtyard, restraining a small sound of alarm as the tall, slim figure in breeches uncoiled from a sack of grain. Were it not for the plait of red hair Gobnait might have been Patrick come again. Fanny had almost abandoned any notion of matching her older sister with anybody. Gobnait spent her days on the moor with her horses, her evenings polishing tackle and poring over bloodlines. Fanny suspected that she even took the occasional nip of whisky.

'Will you see to Belle?' she asked now.

'Be glad to. Did you get your business done?'

'Everything. Profits are up again so I can think about raising the wages.'

'Better not raise them too fast,' Gobnait said dryly. 'We don't want the weavers to get a rush of gold to the head.'

Fanny sent her a frowning look, but the day was too bright for quarrelling, so she turned it into a smile and went briskly through to the kitchen. Her mother, an apron tied over her black gown, was there, the baby against her shoulder as she talked to Huldah, but the conversation broke off as Fanny came in.

'Am I interrupting?' She looked from one to the other.

'Of course not, dear.' Fausty had reddened slightly. 'It's only that—you—you may have heard.'

'Heard what?' Fanny took off her bonnet and reached for the baby. He felt warm and cuddlesome, the big fleecy shawl wrapped about him.

'Henry Ashton is to marry Elizabeth Grant,' Huldah said. 'It's announced in the *Mercury*.'

Elizabeth to wed Henry? Fanny digested the information. It would have been more fitting if Elizabeth had pined for Patrick for the rest of her days, but Elizabeth had never had much sense of what was fitting.

'I wish them both joy,' she said at last. 'Elizabeth will be mistress of Ashton House one day, I suppose.'

'Unless the Ashtons relent towards Philip,' Fausty ventured.

But if they did that then Philip would come home with Esther clinging to his arm. Better that he should remain in Italy, unforgiven. For answer she gave a shrug and a smile that conveyed nothing and walked, still holding the baby, through to the hall. Fausty had looked trim and pretty, the apron neat about her waist, no trace of grey in her black hair. It was as well the young man had not followed. He would have been disillusioned to find out that his 'charming' lady was a grandmother.

Fanny had laid her cheek for a moment against the baby's head, feeling love rise up in her, warm and sweet.

Larch Sabre—he had a right to the name as Fausty had legally adopted him—would grow up to be as fine and brave a gentleman as his grandfather had been. Her arms tightened about him and as her eyes fell on the portrait, visible through the half-open door of the dining-room, Sabre's child drew a long sigh of contented triumph.

We hope you have enjoyed this Large Print book. Other Chivers Press or Thorndike Press Large Print books are available at your library or directly from the publishers.

For more information about current and forthcoming titles, please call or write, without obligation, to:

Chivers Press Limited
Windsor Bridge Road
Bath BA2 3AX
England
Tel. (01225) 335336

OR

Thorndike Press
P.O. Box 159
Thorndike, Maine 04986
USA
Tel. (800) 223-2336

All our Large Print titles are designed for easy reading, and all our books are made to last.